TROUBLE TOWN

By Steve Brewer

Copyright 2021 by Steve Brewer

This is a work of fiction. Any resemblance to real people, living or dead, is coincidental.

For more about the author, check out www.stevebrewer.blogspot.com.

Chapter 1

Some people love to watch poker on television, but in person it's not much of a spectator sport, especially from across the room.

From my post by the front door, it was fifteen feet to the poker table, where six rich guys played hand after hand of Texas Hold 'em. I couldn't see the cards from where I sat, but I had a general idea of who was winning and losing, based on the gloating and the groaning.

Like me, the poker players wore short-sleeved shirts and jeans and sneakers – their weekend clothes – but their jeans were pressed and their sneakers looked new. The men looked like they'd be more comfortable in business suits, their workday armor.

They'd introduced themselves when they arrived for the game, and I'd recognized the names – an ever-smiling member of the Albuquerque City Council, a dour judge, a silver-haired banker, a plump car dealer famed for doing his own TV commercials.

Most notable was Burt "Goatface" Odell, a shady businessman who owned pawn shops and porn shops and strip joints and clip joints all over town.

Odell was balding and he wore thick glasses over brown eyes set so far apart, he could almost look into his own ears. His face was long and narrow, with a waggling wattle under his receding chin. He seemed out of place among the big shots, but they fully accepted him, likely because he was the richest man at the poker table. Crime pays.

Tonight's host was the youngest of the men by twenty years, and he wore white tennis shorts and an aloha shirt decorated with pink flamingos. Gary Pierce was a real estate agent, a fast-talking striver facing his fortieth birthday, which made him a few years younger than me. He looked tan and healthy, and he had perfect teeth and a full head of sun-streaked hair. He drove a red Corvette. He could've been the poster child for mid-life crisis.

The game was at a luxury home Gary had listed for sale. The million-dollar house was a flat-roofed adobe rambler in the leafy neighborhood near the Albuquerque Country Club. The four-bedroom house had curtains, but no furniture except for what had been brought in for the game – the green-felt poker table and a six-foot folding table covered with a nice buffet of meats and cheeses and crackers. The players mostly ignored the food, despite Gary's urgings to eat.

The chairs around the poker table were cushioned armchairs that swiveled, but I was perched on a wooden stool that forced me to stay alert. Any dozing, and I'd fall right over. Whenever I felt myself nodding, I remembered the three hundred bucks I'd collect at the end of the evening. Money always perks me up.

My business card says "Wilton F. 'Bubba' Mabry, Confidential Investigations," but I often pick up side gigs like tonight's door-security job. A man who owns a firearm can always find work.

The other hired hand in the room was Roz Tate, a stout, fifty-something blonde who'd been a professional card dealer for twenty years. I'd never met her before this game, but I admired the way she managed the table while hardly saying a word.

The men had been noisy at first, yakking about the September heat (we were in the annual dry spell between when it rains on the State Fair and when it rains on the Balloon Fiesta) and the coming 2012 presidential election (none of them seemed to care for President Obama, but they liked his opponent less). The chatter diminished once the game got going and the men focused on their cards. It was so quiet in the vacant house, you could hear every snap of a dealt card, every clack of a poker chip.

Quiet as it was, we never heard the robbers coming.

The first indication of the holdup was an enormously loud *crack* as the wooden front door was rammed open. I was so surprised by the noise, I froze there on my stool, not even trying to go for the revolver holstered at my hip.

I wouldn't have succeeded, anyway. The first masked man through the door was carrying a stubby shotgun, and he tipped it up and hit me squarely in the forehead with the butt. Next thing I knew, I was flat on my back on the hardwood floor and the robbers had taken my pistol from its holster and my phone from my shirt pocket.

I raised up on an elbow, dazed and blinking, to see two masked men pointing shotguns at the poker players. A third one aimed a black Glock in my direction. Black ski masks covered everything but their eyes, and they were dressed in matching clothes – long-sleeve black T-shirts, blue jeans, black sneakers and blue latex gloves. They were average-sized guys, but they looked fit and muscular and perfectly capable of kicking the shit out of me.

The battering ram lay on the floor where they'd dropped it, amid wood splinters and plaster dust. The ram was a three-foot length of steel beam with handles welded onto the sides, heavy enough to tear the dead-bolt lock right out of the door frame.

The break-in happened so fast, none of the poker players even tried to rise from their seats. Still, one of the shotgun robbers yelled, "Freeze! Freeze!" and the other shouted, "Nobody move!"

Judge Milton Green, the only African-American in the poker game, instinctively lifted his hands to show they were empty. The others kept their hands visible on the table. They scowled, but said nothing.

The robber with the Glock carried a burlap bag and I suspected my gun and phone had gone in there. He held the bag open as he approached the table.

"All your valuables," he said. "Put 'em in the bag. Wallets, watches, jewelry. And your cell phones."

The men did as they were told, muttering and frowning as they removed their watches and wrested rings off their fingers.

Roz Tate maintained her seen-it-all-before air as the robber progressed around the table. Near her feet sat a small gray lockbox full of cash used to buy chips at the beginning of the game. The buy-in had been a thousand dollars per player, so that metal box held at least six thousand dollars. For a second, I thought the robbers might overlook the box, but no such luck. The one with the Glock put it into the bag with the rest of the loot.

He said to Roz, "The key?"

She dipped a hand inside her white blouse and came up with the lockbox key she'd tucked away there earlier. She handed it over without a word.

The robber got a different reaction when he reached Goatface Odell.

"Do you know who I am?" Odell blurted.

One of the other robbers jabbed the air with his shotgun.

"If you don't shut up, you're gonna be the guy who's gargling buckshot."

Goatface sat still as the gunman went through his pockets, pulling out his phone and his wallet and a thick wad of cash wrapped in a red rubber band. He also found a little flat pistol with pearl grips in Odell's hip pocket. All of it went into the burlap sack.

"You're making a terrible mistake," Odell said.

"I said shut up."

The one with the sack finished up with Sammy Vargas, the car dealer, then he said, "That's it." He twisted the bag shut and backed toward the front door.

"All right," said the thief who had threatened Goatface. "Everybody stay right where you are. Anybody tries to follow us, we'll kill every goddamned one of you."

The trio backed out the door, moving efficiently, keeping us covered. The last one out picked up the battering ram. They slammed the damaged door behind them. The latch no longer worked, but the door stayed shut.

Seconds later, a car engine roared outside and tires screeched on asphalt as the robbers sped away.

Chapter 2

Nobody moved for a few seconds, then noise erupted around the table as the men sputtered and cursed. They jumped up from their chairs, pacing around and shaking the tension out of their arms. Relieved to be alive.

Goatface Odell went to the nearest window and lifted a curtain aside to peek out.

"They're gone," he said. "Nothing's moving out there."

Still dizzy as hell, I clambered to my feet. My forehead throbbed.

The poker players shouted about how surprised they'd been by the robbery. Everyone talked too loud, juiced on adrenaline. Everyone but Roz Tate, who sat silent at the table, and Odell, whose voice came raspy and low.

"How the hell did this happen?" he said to Gary Pierce. "I thought you had this place secured."

Gary stammered, his face glowing, then managed, "Nobody knew we were playing here tonight. And I, uh, I hired a security guard for the door."

All eyes turned to me.

"It happened so fast," I said. "I didn't get a chance to--"

"Worthless," Odell snapped.

I resented that remark, but before I could come up with a rejoinder, City Councilman Carlos Martinez spoke up.

"Who is this guy anyway? Where's Jack?"

They looked to Roz. I knew from what Gary had told me the day before that Jack Tate was her husband, a retired cop who usually worked door security for these Sunday night games.

"He's out of town," Roz said. "His aunt died and he had to go to Tulsa for the funeral."

"Hmm," Odell said, like he didn't quite believe it. "And this was the best replacement we could get?"

Again, the remark stung.

"You weren't exactly Quick Draw McGraw yourself," I said. "You were sitting on a pistol the whole time."

He snorted. "I wasn't being paid to carry a gun. You were."

Councilman Martinez came closer, close enough that I could smell the bourbon on his breath.

"What's your name?"

"Bubba Mabry. I'm a private investigator."

"You're sure as hell not a security guard."

"Look," I said, "I'm sorry this happened. But nobody could've reacted any faster than I did. Not this guy Jack. Not anybody. Boom went the door and, boom again, upside my head."

The men grumbled and cursed, but banker Tom Donovan drowned out the others with his stentorian baritone.

"We can sort out the blame later," he said. "But we need to decide what happens right now."

The men looked at each other, wheels turning behind their eyes. Once again, I made the mistake of speaking up.

"Shouldn't we call the cops?"

"Say what?" said Odell.

"The police? Report the robbery?"

He stepped closer to me. For a second, I thought he'd butt me with his forehead. Like a goat. Instead, he pummeled me with words.

"What are you, stupid?

"Now, wait a min--"

"Private poker games are illegal in New Mexico."

"Technically," interjected Judge Green. "The law's rarely enforced--"

"Doesn't matter," Odell said. "We don't want to give the police any reason to meddle in our affairs. Nobody here wants to end up on the evening news."

The men seemed embarrassed, and they didn't meet Odell's gaze as he looked around the room. Then I got it. These pillars of the community couldn't afford to have their names connected to Goatface Odell and his crime empire. None of them wanted to come right out and say it, but they all knew.

Finally, Vargas, the car dealer, cleared his throat and said, "We couldn't call the cops anyway. They took our phones."

More nods.

"So we just walk away?" Judge Green said. "Act like this never happened?"

"No way," Goatface said. "Nobody steals from me and gets away with it."

Vargas touched his pencil-thin mustache, as if making sure it was still there.

"What then?" he said. "The robbers wore masks and gloves. We have no idea who they were."

"I'll put the word out to all the pawn shops in town," Odell said. "Maybe they'll be stupid enough to try to pawn some of our valuables. Soon as you get home, send me emails, listing everything taken, with good descriptions."

The men nodded, but Vargas still had questions.

"And if the robbers don't go to a pawn shop? What are we supposed to do then?"

Odell turned to me, looking me over with his wide-set eyes.

"You," he said. "You'll find them for us."

"Well, now," I said. "I don't know how I would go about--"

"Didn't you say you were a private investigator?"

I gulped and nodded. No denying it now.

"Then *investigate*. Get me their names, and I'll take care of the rest of it. Nice and quiet."

"And if I can't?"

"Maybe we'll hold *you* responsible for our losses."

He looked around at the other men. He wasn't the tallest or the widest, but he clearly held the most power. Nobody seemed willing to object to this plan.

"That doesn't seem fair," I said. "It wasn't my fault--"

"Yes, it was. You were paid to do a job."

I hadn't been paid yet, but it didn't seem a good time to mention it.

"This is the job now," Goatface said. "Do it quietly, but get it done. Fast."

Chapter 3

Nobody felt like playing poker anymore, and there were credit cards to be canceled, so the men slipped away into the night. Soon, only Gary Pierce and Roz Tate and I remained in the vacant house. Roz was still cool and calm, putting the cards and poker chips away in a metal carrying case. Gary looked shell-shocked, as if he couldn't quite believe what he'd seen.

"You all right?" I asked him.

"This is terrible. This is the worst night of my life."

"C'mon, Gary, it's not that--"

"I've spent four years in this game, mostly losing money, so I could cultivate these guys and their connections. It's cost me a fortune, and now it's all gone. Poof."

"Time will heal it," I offered. "Eventually, they'll stop blaming you."

"No, they won't. They'll probably kick me out of the game because of this one transgression."

"That seems harsh. It's not like *you* robbed them."

"I was the host," he said. "I was the one who said having the game in one of my listed houses was a good idea."

"It *was* a good idea. But somehow, those robbers found out about it."

Gary gaped at me.

"Somebody must've blabbed about the game," I said. "Probably an accident. Somebody mentioned it to someone who mentioned it to somebody else. Eventually, the wrong guys heard about it."

"It wasn't me," Gary said. "I told no one other than the people in the game. And I didn't give them the address until yesterday, right after I told it to you on the phone."

A flash in my scrambled brain: *I shouldn't be so quick to jump on jobs offered at the last minute.*

"One of the other players then," I said. "Somebody let it slip."

Gary and I turned toward the poker table, where Roz snapped shut the metal case.

"Don't look at me," she said. "Jack and I have strict rules against discussing our work with anyone. We make a nice living in retirement, working a few games a week around town. We wouldn't mess that up, blabbing about it."

I nodded. "Jack's in Tulsa, you said?"

"That's right. His aunt's funeral. He'll be back in a day or two."

"And he's been acting normally? Hasn't seemed worried about anything?"

She stood and brushed at the front of her black slacks.

"Jack doesn't worry. Jack makes other people worry. He was a patrol officer for twenty-five years."

"I was just thinking, you know, that these guys wore masks and it might lead someone to wonder if maybe he--"

"Don't be ridiculous," she said. "Jack's in Tulsa. Besides, he's six-foot-four. None of those men was over six feet tall."

"That's true," I said. "You can't fake height. But maybe someone heard he was going to be out of town?"

"I don't see how. We didn't know he was leaving town until two days ago, when we got word that the old lady died."

My headed pounded, but I kept coming up with questions.

"Did everyone around the poker table seem about the same as usual?"

Roz and Gary nodded.

"Nobody seemed nervous? Or, like they were waiting for something?"

They shook their heads.

"Anything about the intruders seem familiar? The way they were built? Their clothes? Their voices?"

"All I could see," Roz said, "were those guns."

Gary sighed. "This isn't helping."

"I'm just getting started," I said.

"Why don't you help me clean up this buffet while you're asking questions?"

We went over to the six-foot-long table, which was still buried in treats and meats and cheeses. A beer cooler sat on the floor nearby, and I fished out some ice, which I wrapped in a white towel to hold against my throbbing forehead. A plastic garbage can sat on the floor at one end of the table, and Gary raked platters and paper plates into it. I hated to see perfectly good food go to waste, but I didn't say anything.

"That's like throwing money in the trash," he said. "And I'm gonna have to get that front door fixed. That'll cost hundreds of dollars. This is a nightmare."

"C'mon, man," I said. "It'll be okay. You'll see."

I didn't really believe that, but he seemed to need the pep talk. I didn't know Gary that well. I'd done some investigative work for him in the past, hunting down vandals and deadbeats. He'd always seemed like a good guy. I hated to see him crack.

He looked up at me, so much hope in his eyes that it made me cringe.

"You really think so?"

"Sure," I lied.

Chapter 4

It was nearly eleven o'clock by the time I got home, and I expected my wife to be asleep. But lights glowed in the windows of our brick bungalow in an otherwise dark block near Monte Vista Elementary School. Head pounding, I shuffled into the house, fully expecting another lecture from Felicia on why I should stop risking my life being a private detective.

But my beloved was distracted. She crouched on the edge of our squishy blue sofa, poring over stacks of documents weighing down the spindly coffee table. Her horn-rimmed glasses rode on the end of her nose. She was dressed in her usual jeans and sneakers and loose blouse, and her brown hair was pulled back in a haphazard ponytail.

"Honey, I'm home," I said.

Without looking up from her papers, she said, "How was the poker game?"

I sighed. No sense lying about it, not with a big purple lump growing in the center of my forehead.

"I wish I could say it was uneventful. But things went sideways."

She looked up at me.

"Holy shit. What happened to your face?"

"Three masked men robbed the poker game. One of them hit me with the butt of a shotgun."

"Good God, Bubba. You could have a concussion."

"Maybe," I said. "My ears are ringing. I feel a little dizzy."

"And you drove home in this condition?"

"Apparently."

Felicia leaped up from the sofa and grasped my elbow. She steered me into an armchair, then tipped a lampshade to throw light in my face, so she could get a better look at my growing bruise. Squinting made it hurt worse.

"Look at me," she said. "Follow my finger."

She waved her hand back and forth, and I tried to focus on it. I guess I passed the test, because she said, "Your eyes look okay. And the swelling is on the outside of your skull."

"As near as we can tell."

"You want to go to the hospital?"

"For a bruise? They'd laugh us out of the emergency room. But they'd make us wait nine hours first."

"We should put ice on it."

"Already did."

"We'll do it more."

I sat quietly until she returned from the kitchen with a frozen bag of green peas. Every household in America keeps freezer peas for injuries, right? Does anybody actually eat them? Felicia pressed the freezer-hard bag against my forehead, which hurt. I took the peas away from her and held them in place myself. Gently.

She went back to the kitchen and returned with two ibuprofen and a glass of water. I dutifully chugged them down.

"Was anybody else injured?" she asked.

"No. Everybody sat still while the gunmen took their stuff, including their cell phones. I'm gonna have to get a new phone. What a hassle--"

"Did they take your wallet?"

"No. I guess they figured the security guy didn't have any money. Which is right. I think I've got twenty bucks on me. But they took my gun. There's another five hundred bucks this'll cost me. Being an armed robbery victim is expensive."

"It's assault and battery, too," Felicia said. "What did the police say when they saw that bruise on your head?"

"Um."

"What?"

"We didn't call the police. The poker players didn't want their names to get out in public--"

"Why not?"

See, this is a persistent problem for me. My cases are supposed to be confidential, and the same goes for jobs like this one-night security gig. But Felicia is an ace reporter for the *Albuquerque Gazette*, and she doesn't believe in keeping secrets. I'm in constant risk of seeing my clients on the front page.

"I guess such poker games are technically illegal in New Mexico--"

"Oh, nobody cares about that. They must have some other reason to not involve the police."

"I dunno," I said, stalling. "I was kinda out of it after I got hit in the head."

She narrowed her eyes at me.

"Who was playing in this game?"

"I really didn't catch their names," I lied. "But they were adamant about the robbery staying out of the news."

"Hmm. So they just let the thieves get away with it?"

"Not exactly."

"What does that mean?"

This is how these conversations usually go. My sweetheart is a dogged questioner, and I'm bad at dreaming up stories on the spot. So, we often end up at the truth, which almost never sets me free.

"I'm supposed to look into it," I said. "They think maybe I can get their valuables back."

Felicia crossed her arms and frowned at me.

"How are you supposed to do that?"

"No idea," I said. "But I'll start pursuing it in the morning. For now, I just want to go to bed."

"Probably not a good idea to sleep yet," she said. "If you've got a concussion--"

"I don't. I'm just a knothead. A weary one."

She trailed me as I headed for the bedroom, then stood in the doorway watching as I shed my shoes and clothes.

"Aren't you coming to bed?" I asked.

"I'm deep into the paperwork on a land deal the city is considering. I may work late."

I crawled into the bed and pulled the covers up to my chin.

"Good night," I said, closing my eyes.

"I want to hear more about these poker players in the morning."

I grunted noncommittally.

She switched off the light and closed the bedroom door, leaving me alone with my thoughts and fears. It took me a long time to fall asleep.

Chapter 5

By morning, the lump on my forehead was dark purple, but the throbbing headache had eased to a dull thump. I was in the bathroom, examining the lump in the mirror, when Felicia appeared in the doorway. She still wore the clothes from the night before.

"Pulled an all-nighter, huh?"

She yawned and stretched. "It's the only time I can get any research done."

Newspapers are struggling nationwide, and the *Gazette* is no exception. Layers of layoffs mean that the ones who remain are forced into a lot of roles in the newsroom. Felicia is in her early 40s, which is considered an aged veteran in today's journalism, and she can manage any task they throw at her. All she wants to do is investigate fat cats and crooks (who, in New Mexico, often turn out to be the same people), but such efforts take a back seat to getting out the newspaper every day. Felicia spends a lot of her workday consumed with frustration.

"Did you uncover something?"

"I'm on the verge," she said. "I can feel it."

I knew better than to question such hunches. They were the fuel in Felicia's engine. Once she got rolling on some suspicion, everyone – including her bosses – better get out of the way.

We padded into the kitchen for coffee.

"What about you?" she said as she filled our mugs. "Are you in any shape to go after your robbers?"

"I feel okay. But I don't know where to begin."

"Maybe I could help," she said. "Tell me who was in the game, and I can tell you what I know about them."

"Um." I took a sip of steaming coffee rather than answer. Burned my tongue.

"Come on, Bubba. I'm not gonna write a story about your poker robbery. I can't imagine that I'd even be interested in some guys playing cards on a Sunday night."

I thought the opposite was true. The men around that poker table were exactly the kind of rich guys Felicia loves to topple. When it comes to pillars of the community, she's Samson.

I'd thought of a diversion while I was still in bed, and now was the time to put it into action.

"I'll tell you one name," I said. "The one who's insisting that I do the investigating now."

She eyed me, her fists on her hips, waiting.

"Burt Odell."

"*Goatface*?"

"Ah, you've heard of him."

"No wonder you didn't argue when he put you in charge of the investigation," she said. "Goatface Odell has a reputation for getting his way."

"Exactly--"

"People who cross him have been known to disappear."

"I'm working for him, not against him."

She looked me over, her gaze coming to rest on the lump on my forehead.

"I imagine he doesn't respond well to disappointment, either."

"You think I'll disappoint him?"

"Aw, Bubba. How can this turn out any other way? The bad guys wore masks. They left no fingerprints. Even the police wouldn't be able to solve this one."

"I have my resources," I said, though I might've had trouble listing any at the moment. "I'll find a way."

She pushed up her glasses and grinned at me.

"That's shockingly optimistic, coming from you."

"Maybe it's confidence."

Her smile widened.

"Maybe that'll keep Goatface from vanishing you."

"Here's hoping. At least you'll know where to start looking if I disappear."

Felicia checked the clock over the stove. It was nearly 8 a.m.

"I need to get in the shower," she said. "I want to get to the office before everybody else shows up."

"What about sleep?"

"No time. A shower will wake me up."

I glanced at the level of the coffee in the glass pot.

"How many cups have you had?"

"I don't know. Who's counting?"

As soon as I could hear water running in the bathroom, I went to my office, which occupies what once was the front bedroom.

Years ago, we had a side entrance installed for the office, but it's almost never used. Clients rarely came to see me in person anymore; everything's done by e-mail and text message. I sometimes worked entire cases where I never even met the client.

So different from the dozens of detective paperbacks I've read over the years, which usually open with a luscious potential client slinking into the office and hiring the worldly private eye. Instead of a fedora, I got a knot on my head. Instead of a *femme fatale*, I got Goatface.

Soon as my computer booted up, I searched the internet for information about the poker players. Lots to choose from – newspaper archives, Wikipedia pages, Facebook searches – all the men had large profiles online. All but Goatface, who was understandably absent from LinkedIn and the rest.

Sadly, computer searches are most of what private eyes do these days. All the information in the whole wide world is on the web. When a business wants to vet new hires, for instance, there's no longer any knocking on doors or face-to-face interviews. Just a Google search, from the comfort of my own home. Whoever thought investigating could get so boring?

I jotted a few notes as I went, but I kept my cursor moving, trying to avoid going too deep in my research. It would be easy to spend the whole day down the rabbit hole, hunting information on this many names, but I needed to get out of the house. I needed to go buy a new phone, as Felicia reminded me as she left for the *Gazette*.

After three hours in front of the screen, here's some of what I'd found:

--Most frequently in the news was Carlos Martinez, who was in his second term on the nine-member City Council. Martinez represented part of the West Side, the ever-growing suburbs that climb toward the dead volcanoes on Albuquerque's horizon. Martinez was a middle-of-the-road Democrat with a thousand-watt smile. He seemed good at not stepping on others' toes. His name was being bandied about as a future governor. No wonder he was always smiling.

--Milton Green was the subject of political speculation, too. The long-time District Court judge apparently was next up for a seat on the state Supreme Court. Near as I could tell from my superficial research, Green was as clean as they come, never even a hint of favoritism or controversy. How did he end up regularly playing poker with Goatface Odell?

--Sammy Vargas inherited a car dealership and turned it into a dynasty. Now, Vargas owned three dealerships in Albuquerque as well as outposts in Santa Fe and Gallup. Supposedly, he sold more cars and trucks than anyone else in the state. Of interest to me was that he had branched out from autos the past few years, and had been a partner in a couple of big real estate developments, including at least one involving:

--First State Bank president Tom Donovan, who had his fingers in projects all over town. Donovan appeared to be a millionaire several times over, well past retirement age, but he still was the first one to arrive for work at the bank every day.

--Burt Odell made a few headlines, usually brief stories about how one of his properties had been raided by police. The most recent raid involved a bodega that specialized in cut-rate cosmetics shoplifted from other retailers. Odell owned the building, but the police weren't able to prove he had any knowledge of what his tenants were selling. Other articles were similar. Goatface always seemed just out of reach of the authorities.

While I was at it, I looked up Jack and Roz Tate. I found an address way up in the Northeast Heights, but the only other hit was a Facebook account that hadn't been updated in months. Roz had said they kept their card-game business quiet, and she wasn't kidding.

I did a search on Gary Pierce, too, but it turned up hundreds of advertisements for houses he'd sold. He was all over social media, too, showing off homes most of us could never afford. No wonder he was trying to get in good with the rich folks.

I could understand why the poker game would be attractive to a hustler like Gary, for whom every event is a marketing moment. But what about the other guys around the table? What did they stand to gain from each others' company? What went on at these games besides poker?

Lots of questions, but none more urgent than the Big Question that I was supposed to be answering: Who in these important men's lives had set them up to be robbed at gunpoint?

Chapter 6

I caught sight of myself in a wall mirror as I headed out the door. The purple lump stood out on my forehead like a nascent horn. I turned back for a cap to hide the unicorn effect.

As my lank brown hair has gotten thinner, I've taken to wearing baseball caps to protect my scalp from the relentless New Mexico sun. Like most American guys, I've accumulated a collection, but my favorite is a white-and-red Albuquerque Isotopes cap with its whirling-atoms logo. Our minor-league baseball team became the Isotopes after a public vote years ago, a tip of the cap (as it were) to Albuquerque's large population of science nerds. I don't care anything about baseball, but I like the cap. I gently fit it over my horn and left the house.

I took Indian School Road to Louisiana Boulevard, driving through mostly residential areas. The street corners bristled with campaign signs for the coming election. It was as if someone had spilled red-white-and-blue all over town.

My first stop was a phone store near the Coronado Center shopping mall. The place was jumping, and I had to take a number and wait ten minutes before being assigned to a sales rep. He was an earnest, sweaty young man who smelled faintly of mildew. I explained to him that my phone had been "lost" and that I wanted one just like it as a replacement. He smiled his way through this explanation, then immediately launched into a crusade to get me to upgrade to a bigger phone.

I said I didn't want a bigger phone. I wanted one that would fit in my shirt pocket.

He told me the new 2012 model was great for watching movies.

"I have a television for that," I said.

He said it was easier to navigate the internet with a bigger screen.

"I have a desktop computer for that."

He said the latest phone was faster and more powerful than my favored model.

"I don't care," I said. "I want it to fit in my shirt pocket."

He showed me how he carried his phone in his *hip* pocket, to allow for the new, improved, larger size. I told him I didn't want to sit on my phone.

We went back and forth like this for five minutes before he'd finally run through his arsenal.

"So that's it then?" he said. "Your biggest concern is whether you can fit the phone into your shirt pocket."

"Now you're getting it."

He sighed and went to the back of the store to "find and dust off" my preferred model. I managed not to smirk. The customer's always right.

Fifteen minutes later, updated phone in my shirt pocket, I climbed back into my twenty-year-old Oldsmobile Cutlass, an anonymous gray sedan perfect for my line of work.

I took a moment to text Felicia to let her know she could reach me by phone again, at the same old number, then I cranked the car's starter a few times. More and more, it was hard to start, a problem I'd been trying to ignore.

Once the balky engine caught, the old car had plenty of horsepower. I zoomed out of the parking lot and into the busy streets of Albuquerque.

My next stop was Red's Pool Hall, a windowless concrete bunker way out on East Central Avenue. Red's was a relic of another time, already a seedy dive back when this stretch of road was still called Route 66. Now it was surrounded by claptrap motels and fast-food joints. Inside, a dozen pocket billiard tables were spaced out under pools of light from hanging lamps. You could hide in the shadows at Red's, and that attracted the kind of clientele who preferred to not be seen.

The only brightly lit corner of the place was at the cash register, where the owner perched on a stool all day every day.

Red's namesake hair had long ago turned silver, and his face was creased into a thousand wrinkles. He seemed to get an inch shorter with each passing year. But his mind was sharp as ever, and it was a catalog of Albuquerque crime.

"Hey, Red."

"Bubba Mabry! You old sad sack. How have you been?"

See, he recognized me, even though it had been months since we'd last seen each other. Still sharp as ever.

"Good," I said. "Everything's been going pretty well."

"Yeah? Then what happened to your forehead?"

Oops. I'd pushed the Isotopes cap back when I first stepped into the dim pool hall. Forgot I was covering up my lump. I reset the cap lower over my brows.

"I ran into an armed robbery crew," I said. "One of them knocked me cold with the butt of a shotgun."

Red's wrinkles screwed up into an "ouch" expression, then his face went back to its usual suspicious squint.

"What did you do to piss 'em off?"

"Nothing! I was just sitting by the door."

"Where was this?"

I looked around to see if anyone was listening, but, hell, who could tell? A whole platoon could be hiding in the shadowy corners.

"At a private poker game."

Red's bushy eyebrows shot up.

"Somebody stuck up a kitchen game?"

"The stakes were higher than that, a lot of cash on hand, so they had me watching the door."

Red laughed. "Sounds like you did a stellar job."

"It happened really fast. Anyway, I thought you might have heard something. People trying to unload fancy watches or phones, stuff like that."

More cackling.

"I hear about such things every day. But nothing about a poker game. Sounds like a new crew is working in town. They wear masks?"

I nodded. "Full ski masks, gloves, the works. They were white guys, though."

"How do you know?"

"Their eyelids. Everybody blinks."

Red nodded approvingly. "At least you were paying attention. Pretty good, considering you'd been smacked in the forehead."

He seemed to be enjoying my plight more than necessary. And he had no information for me, so this was becoming an exercise in humiliation without any payoff.

"I gotta go," I said. "But keep your ears open, all right? If you hear anything about a poker game--"

"I've got your number, Bubba."

Only after I'd stumbled out into the dazzling daylight did I recognize he could've meant that a couple of different ways.

I spent the afternoon having similar conversations with a dozen other contacts up and down Central Avenue, and the results were always the same. Nobody had heard anything about this robbery. Nobody knew this crew. Nobody knew anything.

Finally giving up, I headed for home as the sun dipped toward the horizon, making the mountains blush.

I'd planted seeds all over town. Maybe one of the robbers would make a mistake and crow about the recent haul. Maybe somebody would hear about it and call me. Maybe I could track the robbers down from that contact. I knew this weak-ass strategy wouldn't be good enough for Goatface Odell. He wasn't interested in "maybes."

I kept coming back to how the robbers had known to hit a curtained house with a "For Sale" sign in the front yard. Somebody had leaked the location of that poker game. There simply wasn't any other way.

I needed to talk to the poker players individually. Jog their memories. See if one of them could remember letting it slip somewhere.

Too late in the day now. I was weary and my headache had returned. I resolved to get after that part of the investigation first thing in the morning.

Chapter 7

Felicia was already home when I got there. She, too, was exhausted after her sleepless night and a full day of work. She sprawled on the sofa, her eyelids at half-mast, a half-empty Heineken bottle in her hands. I got a beer of my own and flopped onto the blue sofa next to her.

She grunted a hello and I responded in kind. Then we drank in silence for a minute, decompressing.

"Busy day?" she said finally.

"The busiest."

"Making progress?"

"None," I admitted.

Another grunt, which somehow managed to communicate that she had expected as much.

"You?"

She sighed. "I spent the day acting as assistant city editor because Jocelyn was out sick. I edited other people's terrible copy. I answered the phone. I argued with idiots."

"You always make it sound like such fun."

Grunt.

I drained my beer and sat up straight.

"Whew," I said. "That's better. You want dinner?"

"Too tired to chew."

"Want another beer?"

"Definitely."

I lurched to my feet and shuffled off to the kitchen. I was bent over, halfway into the fridge, reaching to where the beers stood behind some other stuff, when a sudden shriek jolted me, causing me to whack the back of my head on the inside of the refrigerator.

A pause, long enough for me to curse and jerk backward, then another inarticulate shriek. It sounded like someone killing a small animal in some terrible way. Only when it broke off again did I realize the noise was coming from my own shirt pocket.

Quick thoughts: *That's my new phone. That idiot salesman set my ringtone to some unrecognizable death-metal song with a shrieking singer. His little revenge for me being such a smart-ass. How do I make it stop? How do I change it? Wait a second. If that's the ringtone, then that means I'm getting a **call**.*

I punched the green button on the phone's face and said, "Hello?"

"Bubba Mabry?"

"Yes?"

I took a deep breath, trying to get hold of myself.

"Do you know who this is?"

A man's voice. Deep and raspy, but with an old-man warble. Kind of a bleat.

"Mr. Odell?"

"Don't say names on the phone, you idiot."

It was Goatface all right.

"Yes, sir."

I closed the refrigerator door. This could take a minute.

"You making any progress?" he asked.

"Well, sir, that's hard to say."

"You have the names of those men?"

"Not yet."

"Then that's no progress at all."

"I've put the word out all over town," I said.

"What does that even mean?"

"I have a network among the local criminal element," I said. "Friends, people I've cultivated over the years. They're all keeping their ears open, in case one of these guys gets sloppy, talking in a bar or something like that."

"You spent the day going to bars?"

"Partly. Crooks tend to congregate in bars."

Goatface harrumphed.

"I've got no respect for drunks," he said. "I'm a teetotaler. Sober more than thirty years now."

"Uh-huh." I opened the fridge and bent over and reached again for the beers in the back.

"I wouldn't have asked you to investigate this," Goatface said, "if I'd known you were a drunk."

Whack! I hit my head on the fridge again.

"*I'm* not a drunk," I protested, as I freed the beers from captivity. "I only go into these places to ask about criminal activity."

"Is that what you tell your wife?"

"*What?*"

"I didn't really know who you were last night, but I put it together today. Your wife is that reporter at the *Gazette*."

"True, but--"

"I hope you know better than to mention the poker game to her."

"All my investigations are confidential."

Goatface scoffed. I thought it would be wise to change the subject.

"I keep coming back to the idea of that vacant house," I said. "Somebody must've leaked the location of the poker game."

"We've been playing together for years," Goatface said. "Everybody knows to keep the location a secret."

"The players probably talk about it more than anyone lets on," I said. "They tell their wives where they're going. Or their secretary has it penciled on their calendars. Something like that. The wrong person gets hold of that information--"

"Listen to yourself," he said. "You're talking about tracking our every move leading up to the game? Six, seven people?"

"Maybe everybody could re-examine their own conversations, see if there's anything there to indicate a slip."

"Don't look at me," Goatface said. "I know how to keep my mouth shut."

"Yes, sir."

"What about you, Mr. Private Eye? How do we know *you* weren't the one who blabbed it somewhere?"

"I didn't know about the game until Saturday. And I didn't know it was a high-stakes game until I got there on Sunday. Gary Pierce had said it was just a friendly game."

"It *is* a friendly game," he said. "Or it was. I don't know now. Depends on what you find out."

I had both icy beer bottles in one hand, holding them by their necks, but I didn't want to return to the living room until this conversation was over. I peeked around the corner, checking on Felicia, but she appeared to be dozing on the sofa.

"Look," I said into the phone. "Those guys seemed like professionals, so it's unlikely they'll slip up now. They'll keep quiet. They won't make any kind of move until they're sure nobody's onto them. Maybe they'll move the goods out of state--"

"No. That's unacceptable. I want you to find them before they have a chance to fence those valuables."

"I'm doing the best I can--"

"Do more. Do it faster."

I sighed.

"Sober up," he snarled, "and get to work."

The call clicked off. I stared at my new phone for a second, making sure we were disconnected, then I pocketed the phone and carried the beers into the living room.

"Who was that?" Felicia asked sleepily.

"Business call."

"Hmm. And that shrieking sound?"

"My new ringtone."

"Interesting choice."

"The phone salesman set it up for me. His idea of a joke."

"Ah."

"I'll change it," I said. "Right after this beer."

Chapter 8

Tuesday, I was up bright and early, ready to chase down the poker players and interview them. I started with Judge Milton Green, mostly because I knew where to find him at nine o'clock on a weekday morning.

The Second Judicial District Court building faces Lomas Boulevard downtown. Six stories tall, the courthouse is a limestone tower with lots of windows and curves and it's capped with rounded blue roofs, so it looks like a mid-price hotel.

Judge Green's daily docket was already under way by the time I cleared the lobby metal detectors and found my way upstairs to his courtroom. I slipped into a pew at the back of the congregation and waited for him to notice me there. I'd removed my cap, as required in court, and anyone could spot my bruised lump across a crowded room.

I could tell right away that he saw me. His impassive face twisted into a frown. I often have that effect on people. The judge gestured a uniformed bailiff over to his bench and leaned over to whisper to him. The bailiff, a beefy redhead, looked right at me.

Uh-oh.

"The court will take a ten-minute recess," Judge Green abruptly announced. He stood and disappeared through a side door in a rustle of black robes.

The bailiff made a beeline for me. I stood, but there was no getting away. He grabbed me by the elbow.

"The judge wants to see you in chambers."

I tried to wrest my arm loose, but his grip was firm.

"Okay," I said. "Let's go there."

He marched me across the courtroom to where Green had exited. My shoulder slammed against the jamb as we went through the door; I don't think it was an accident, either. Before I could protest, I got a look at the scowl on Judge Green's face. I decided silence would be the safer course.

"Thank you, Brian," Green said to the bailiff. "That'll be all."

The redhead gave my elbow a departing squeeze – which hurt – then left me alone with the judge, who sat behind a mahogany desk, still in his robe. The walls were mostly wooden bookshelves packed with fat law tomes. On the wall behind him hung several photos of Judge Green shaking hands with President Obama and the First Lady and other dignitaries. A couple of empty chairs faced his desk, but I was not invited to sit.

"The fuck are you doing in my courtroom, Mabry?"

That didn't sound particularly judicial, but I could tell he was riled. I twisted my Isotopes cap in my hands.

"I wanted to talk to you, so I--"

"I can't be seen with you. Someone could use you to tie me to the poker games."

"I don't see how--"

"There's probably a lot you don't see."

"You don't have to be so--"

"What do you *want,* Mabry?"

"I'm trying to talk to everybody in the game. To ask if they might've mentioned the game's location to anyone beforehand."

"Why would anyone do that?"

"Right. Then how did those robbers know we'd be there? Somebody told somebody something. I'm trying to backtrack--"

"I never spoke of the game to anyone," he said. "I never have. It's my personal secret."

"You didn't mention it to your wife?"

"I'm divorced," he said. "I live alone."

"Maybe you mentioned it to your bailiff? Secretary? A note on your calendar? Or on your computer?"

Judge Green shook his head until I ran out of steam.

"You're wasting my time," he said.

I had one more question. "Why do you even play in those games, if they're so risky to your reputation?"

The judge took a deep breath. Finally, an answer other than "no."

"It's because of Burt," he said. "We've known each other forty years, since our undergrad days at UNM. We were in the same dorm. We became friends. Allies. The bookish black kid and the funny-looking white kid. We got each other through some tough times."

He paused, staring at the top of his desk.

"Your paths diverged as you got older," I said.

He nodded.

"Completely. But we managed to remain friends. We still enjoy each other's company."

I couldn't imagine that spending time with Goatface would be much fun, but maybe I hadn't seen that side of his personality yet.

"Time's up," Green said. "I've got to get back into the courtroom."

"Sure. That's all the questions I had anyway. I knew it would only take a minute--"

"Go out the other door," he said. "I don't want you traipsing through my courtroom. In fact, Mabry, I never want to see you again. Ever. Clear?"

That seemed harsh, but I nodded and scooted out of there.

Chapter 9

City Hall was only three blocks away, so I left my car where it was parked and walked over. The September sun beat down on my shoulders and I was glad I had my Isotopes cap to shade my face. I was dressed in my usual getup – sunglasses and faded jeans and dusty sneakers and a blue Hawaiian shirt loose enough to conceal a gun when I carried one.

Which reminded me: I needed to replace my stolen pistol. A private eye can't walk around unarmed. It's unseemly.

As I cut across the sun-baked expanse of Civic Plaza, I called ahead to the office of City Councilman Carlos Martinez. A secretary said the councilman's calendar was full.

"Tell him Bubba Mabry needs five minutes. He'll squeeze me in. Trust me."

"Did you say 'Bubba?'"

"That's right."

"Can you spell that?"

I sighed. But I spelled it. Spelled my last name, too, while I was at it. Felt like an idiot, out walking around in the sunshine, spelling stuff, but such is life in 2012. The world is your phone booth.

She put me on hold so long, I was nearly to the doors of City Hall by the time she came back on and said Councilman Martinez might have five minutes to spare after all.

Gun-free, I sailed through Security. I caught an elevator as the door was closing. Within minutes I was standing in front of the secretary who'd been on the phone. I knew it was her because my name was printed in big, loopy letters on a pink Post-It near her elbow.

I identified myself, which made her frown, as if she hadn't expected me so soon. She pointed to the other side of the anteroom, where three unarmed chairs were lined up against the wall. She told me to sit and wait.

I sat and waited.

Fifteen minutes later, the door to the interior office opened and a plump old lady tottered out. She wore a wide-brimmed red hat with matching red shoes and handbag. Her powdered face was set in a satisfied smile. I got the impression she'd just told off her city councilman and was proud of the effort.

Martinez, dressed in a dark suit and tie, filled the doorway behind her, a big smile on his face until the old lady was out of sight. Then he scowled at me and crooked his finger to show I should join him in the inner sanctum.

By the time I got to my feet and followed him through the door, he was already behind his desk. The wall behind him was mostly glass, looking out at other downtown high-rises and the Sandia Mountains beyond. This sort of view always catches me by surprise. I live at street level in Albuquerque. I forget that the fat cats inhabit a different city, up above the rest of us, making laws and cutting deals.

"What can I do for you, Mr. Mabry?"

Martinez was smiling again, but it was a tight smile, not showing his bright teeth. His hands rested on his desk. No fidget there at all. If he was worried about me being here, he didn't show it. I reminded myself that Martinez and the rest were poker players, accustomed to maintaining a straight face no matter the cards dealt.

I explained how I suspected a leak, and that I was asking each of the players to examine the twenty-four hours leading up to the game in search of some inadvertent slip.

"Well, it wasn't me," Martinez said. "The game's privacy has always been paramount to me. Last thing I need is to come out of the game and find a news crew waiting in ambush."

I nodded. "Maybe just take a minute and think back over your recent conversations--"

"I probably talked to thirty or forty people during that time. As you can see--"

He turned a computer tablet on his desk so that I could see the screen. It showed the day's appointments. Every color-coded slot was full, well into the evening.

"--I have no free time, Mr. Mabry. I am always 'on.' Which means I'm always, and I mean *always*, watching what I say."

"Sure, but anybody could make a mistake. You know, joking around with your wife. Or leaving a message on your phone where someone could see--"

"Not me," Martinez said. "I'm the most careful politician you're ever going to meet."

He gave me the high-beams smile.

"I'm going places, Mr. Mabry. I have ambitions."

I nodded, remembering the online speculation about a run for the governor's mansion.

"You don't succeed in politics by speaking out of turn," he said. "You have to measure every word."

"All right, all right," I said, exasperated. "If not you, then who?"

Martinez swiveled in his chair, showing me his manly profile as he stared out the window, thinking it over. He looked like he should be on a coin.

"If I had to bet on someone," he said, "I'd pick Gary Pierce."

That surprised me. "Really? Why?"

He swiveled back around to face me, his lips barely moving as he said, "Understand, this is complete speculation on my part."

"Yeah, yeah. Why?"

"Well, Gary's the youngest of us, you know, and he's always trying to impress the other guys, talking about luxury homes he's sold."

I nodded. I'd always gotten a similar vibe from Gary.

"He likes to talk," I said.

"He does. Also, having the game at that vacant house was his idea. It seemed a little creepy to me, frankly. We usually play in someone's dining room. The game moves around every week. Hard for anyone to predict where we might be. The TV stations aren't likely to stake out six different houses, hoping to stumble across our little game."

That smile again, as if the very mention of television caused it to automatically bloom. Speaking of vacant and creepy.

"If Gary had to make arrangements for us to use that house," Martinez said, "then someone at his office might've figured out that it was for the poker game. And Gary no doubt has told them in the past that he's a high-roller."

"No doubt."

"A secretary or another real estate agent hears about his scheduling of the vacant house, puts two and two together--"

"And comes up with three robbers."

That broad smile again. I wished he'd stop wasting it on me. Save it for the campaign trail.

"I think you're onto something, Mr. Mabry. If I were you, I'd pursue that angle."

"All right. Thanks."

"Now, if you don't mind?"

He pointed at the schedule on his computer screen.

"I've probably put you way behind," I said. "Thanks for your time."

I stumbled out of there, my mind whirring. Martinez had made it sound like it was my idea to suspect Gary, but it had come from him. He'd directed our conversation the whole way, smooth-talking his ideas into my lumpy head.

But what he said about Gary wasn't wrong. He *was* a blabbermouth; it was his stock-in-trade. He'd talk your ear off, right up to the moment you found yourself signing a huge mortgage. Then he'd go find some other ear to bend.

Maybe he spoke into the wrong ear this time. I needed to go see him next.

Chapter 10

When I phoned Gary Pierce, he agreed to see me right away. He was back at the scene of the poker game, waiting on a crew to repair the battered front door.

I parked at the curb behind a white van covered with advertisements for a handyman service. Two guys in gray coveralls were at work on the front porch, replacing the door frame that had been splintered the night of the stickup.

Through the front windows, I could see Gary in the empty living room, pacing back and forth, his phone to his ear. The sleeves of his white shirt were rolled up to his elbows, showing off the tennis tan on his forearms. His sun-streaked hair was pushed back from his face, like he'd been running his hands through it.

Muttering "excuse me," I squeezed between the guys working on the door and went inside. Gary saw me and held up a finger to show me to wait.

"That's not good enough," he said into the phone. "If you can't come up with the full amount up front, then the deal's off. The current owner was very specific--"

Gary held the phone out from his face and looked at it, frowning. Clearly, whoever had been on the other end had hung up. He pocketed the phone and turned to me, not even bothering to turn on the expensive smile he showed off in his newspaper ads.

"What do *you* want?"

There was no need to take such a tone, but Gary seemed exasperated, and here I was, a convenient scapegoat.

"Aren't you supposed to be out catching robbers?"

I gave him a shushing look and glanced over at the workmen by the front door. They didn't appear to be listening to us. One of them was lining up a power drill, and the sudden shriek of penetrated wood drowned out whatever Gary said next.

"I need to talk to you in private," I said when the noise stopped.

Gary led me into the next room, which was a dining room with a wall of windows looking out at the back lawn. In the sunlight streaming through the windows, I could see that Gary had circles under his eyes. Worry written across his forehead.

"You all right?" I asked.

"No, I'm not *all right*--"

He caught himself. Clamped his lips shut and took a deep breath through his nose, pulling himself together. I tried to look concerned and sympathetic, but I'm not sure it came across. My face sometimes lets me down.

"I'm fine," he said. "I just had a sale fall through, and I'd been counting on the commission. But I've got other people interested in that property. It'll be okay."

I nodded along, but I thought something else was troubling him. And it probably had to do with me.

"Have you heard anything from the other poker players?" I said, trying for a diversion. "Any news?"

"Oh, I've been hearing from people all right. Judge Green, for one. He was not happy that you showed up in his courtroom."

"I got that impression."

"And you went to City Hall, too? You know everybody who goes in and out of there is photographed, right?"

I actually hadn't given it much thought. I shrugged.

"They've got cameras everywhere, Bubba."

I wondered exactly who he meant by "they," but that seemed an unproductive tangent at the moment.

"So Martinez called you, too?" I asked.

"Gave me a chewing-out I didn't deserve, then hung up before I could say a word."

"Ouch."

He sighed and looked around the empty room.

"Worst idea I've ever had," he said. "Hosting the poker game here."

"You had no way of knowing those thieves would show up."

It wasn't a question, but I still watched him closely for a response, looking for any sign of guilt. Had he mentioned the game to someone? Had he come to realize it since? But his expression didn't change. He looked beleaguered and bewildered, like he'd been steamrolled by life and was trying to unflatten himself.

"When those guys bashed open the door," he said, "I nearly pissed myself."

"That never helps anything."

"Pissing yourself?"

"That's been my experience."

Gary looked like he was ready to pursue that further, then he shook his head and changed the subject.

"Are you making any progress at all?"

"Some," I said. "Talking to different people. Ruling things out. Process of elimination and all that."

He almost managed to keep the sneer out of his voice as he said, "Investigating."

"That's right. Good old-fashioned legwork. Asking questions and seeing where the answers lead."

"And where have they led you so far?"

"Right back here. How did those guys know to hit the game at this vacant house? I mean, they clearly were prepared. They had the matching ski masks and the guns and that battering ram."

Gary made a face, like what I was saying was obvious. Maybe it was. But it was clicking together in my head as I said it out loud.

"So they had that gear together ahead of time," I said. "When they found out the game was here at this house, it must've seemed the perfect opportunity. But how did they find out?"

Gary glanced into the living room to make sure we weren't being overheard by the workmen.

"Maybe they followed somebody here," he said.

"That's possible," I said. "But why did they wait two hours before bashing in the door?"

"Maybe they were waiting for night to fall. They were dressed in black. They didn't want the neighbors to see."

I nodded. That made sense.

"Did you mention the game to anyone in your office?" I asked.

Gary looked away, like he was trying to remember. Or trying to hide something.

"No," he said. "I was very careful about that. Nobody knew people were coming to this house for poker. We haven't opened the house to other agents yet. I'm the only one with a key."

"You got here early?"

"Yeah, you know, to set up the refreshments and stuff. I was here nearly an hour before Roz showed up."

"She was the first to arrive?"

"Yeah. Very professional. Said hardly anything beyond 'hello.' Just started counting out the poker chips and stuff."

"Did you have reason to look outside when she arrived? Any sign she was being followed? Or that somebody was watching the house?"

"I was in and out a lot, going out to my car," he said. "I never saw anything suspicious."

"Hmm. Maybe I need to talk to Roz again. Of all the people at the table, she seemed the least surprised when those guys burst in."

"She's a cool customer," Gary said. "Hard to rattle her."

"Maybe somebody followed her," I said. "She does other games around town, right? Maybe they followed her for days, waiting for the right location."

Gary looked skeptical.

"Don't get me wrong," I said. "I still think there's a better chance that the robbers were alerted ahead of time. You've never mentioned the game to *anyone*? One of your tennis buddies?"

"That's the only rule of this game," he said. "Absolute secrecy. Mess that up some way, and you're out."

He looked glum.

"It'll be okay," I said. "If it turns out that somebody else led the robbers to the game, you'll be off the hook."

He nodded, but he didn't seem to feel any better. Maybe he didn't think my investigative abilities were up to the job. I'm familiar with such doubt.

"It may turn out that no one in the game is really at fault," I said.

"I don't think Burt Odell will see it that way."

"He called me," I said. "Made it clear he wants results right away."

Gary nodded. "He's worried about his phone."

"His phone?"

"Burt uses that phone for business," he said. "It would be bad if it fell into the wrong hands."

Took me a second, but I soon realized the "wrong hands" would be the ones attached to the long arms of the law. The police have a word for the user history recorded on cell phones: "Evidence."

"That could be a valuable phone," I said. "If the robbers are arrested, they could use it as a bargaining chip."

"It would be a 'get out of jail free' card," he agreed. "Worth more to the police than any armed robbery case."

I thought it over for a second, then said, "That only works if the robbers know whose phone they've got. All the phones went into that burlap sack. And the robbers didn't seem to recognize Goatface."

Gary recoiled at the nickname, then continued as if he hadn't heard it.

"You could see why Burt might be worried about that phone," he said. "It's a risk floating around out there. He doesn't like risks."

"I thought he liked poker. Isn't that all about risks?"

"Not the way Burt plays it. He's always calculating the odds, counting the cards. He's usually two or three steps ahead of the rest of us."

"I'll remember that," I said. "Next time I talk to him."

"You'd better make it soon. Burt doesn't like waiting, either."

I sighed. "Nobody does."

Chapter 11

Felicia's sun-bleached Toyota was in the driveway when I got home, which surprised me. She usually works through lunch.

I went up the front steps and unlocked the door and stepped inside, preparing a smile for my sweetie. She was on the sofa, awash in a sea of documents that bore circles and slashes and arrows drawn with a blood-red marker. Her eyeglasses had slipped down, and her brown eyes seemed sort of glazed.

"Oh, it's you," she said. "Hi."

That gave me pause. "You were expecting someone else?"

"No, I was just lost in thought. I've got all these puzzle pieces and I'm trying to fit them together."

She gestured at the legal papers all around her. The sight of that much boilerplate gave me the willies.

"You know anything about deeds?" she asked.

"'Deed I do."

"Really?"

"No. I was just kidding around."

"Do I look like I'm kidding?"

She did not.

"I can see you're working," I said. "I'll just go in the kitchen and make myself a quick sandwich. Quietly."

"Make two," she said. "I'm starving."

I slapped together a couple of ham sandwiches and opened a fresh bag of potato chips. I put it all on the round table in our little dining room, which connects the living room and kitchen through arched doorways. Once everything was in place, I announced, "Luncheon is served."

Felicia set some papers aside and tried to stand, but her attention was still riveted to the page. Finally, she shook her head to break the spell and came to the dining room.

"Beer?" I asked.

"Yes, please."

I got two Heinekens out of the back of the fridge (without hitting my head) and cracked them open before I brought them to the table.

Felicia still seemed entranced by the pile of papers, but the beer got her attention.

"I thought you were working," she said.

"I am. And my total lack of progress deserves a beer."

She pointed at her paperwork in the next room. "Same here."

We munched and sipped and swallowed for a few minutes without talking, but I knew we'd eventually get around to my investigation.

"Where were you all morning?" she asked finally.

"Downtown," I said. "Trying to talk to the poker players, trying to see if anyone might've told someone about the location of the secret game."

"And?"

"Everybody says they weren't the ones to leak it," I said. "Of course."

"Of course."

She crunched a potato chip. Her eyes were focused on a blank spot on the opposite wall. I knew that look. Her brain was busy processing, forming questions, making connections. Her brain works twice as fast as mine, which means I nearly always lose the argument.

"When you say 'downtown,' do you mean at City Hall or the cop shop?"

"Certainly not police headquarters," I said. "I'm under strict orders to keep the cops out of this."

"Right," she said. "Who do you know at City Hall?"

"Um."

"Oh, Bubba. Don't make me worm it out of you. It'll ruin your lunch break."

She was frustrated with her mountain of paperwork, and she'd quite willingly take her frustrations out on me. The dodgier my answers, the more questions she'd ask. She *would* worm it out of me. It probably wouldn't even take that long. I was already in a weakened condition, what with my forehead lump and my lunchtime beer.

I sighed.

"I was at City Hall to see Councilman Carlos Martinez. Okay? No big deal."

"He's one of the poker players?"

"Yes. Happy now?"

"He plays poker with *Goatface*?"

"Uh."

"Every *week*?"

"And some other guys. It's not just Goatface--"

But she was headed a different direction. "You just waltzed into Martinez's office and you got to see him?"

"I called ahead--"

"He must be worried about you," she said.

"Me?"

"Why else would he agree to see you? I've been trying to get an interview with him for two weeks and he never has a spare moment."

"Sounds to me," I said, "like he must be worried about *you*."

She scoffed.

"Why are you trying to interview him?" I asked.

"This land development deal I've been looking into?"

"Yeah?"

"It's in his City Council district."

"Ah."

Frowning, she downed more beer. When she came up for air, I said, "Something's fishy about it?"

Fire sparked in her eyes. Sometimes, I wish I could excite Felicia the way a hot story does.

"I can't prove it yet," she said. "I can't even prove who owns the land in question. Somebody has buried it under piles of bullshit."

"Like what?"

"Dummy corporations, land grants, competing claims, variances, the works. This tract had been tied up in the courts for years. Suddenly, the path has been cleared for Sammy Vargas and his bunch to build a subdivision there with fifty upscale homes. They're calling it Milagro Estates."

I tried to maintain my poker face at the mention of Vargas' name, but I must've failed because Felicia said, "What?"

"Where is this?"

"Just the other side of the river, not far from the existing Open Space park. I took you over there last year?"

"The place with the sandhill cranes? Great view of the mountains?"

"Right."

"It's all cottonwoods and alfalfa fields. They want to put a bunch of houses there?"

She took her time, touching her napkin to her lips and pushing her plate aside before she said, "That's what they *want* us to think."

I pondered that for a moment, then said, "I have no idea what you mean."

"It's this bait-and-switch thing developers do in this town," she said. "They take some land that's valuable only because the city wants to preserve it as open space or turn it into a park. Then they act like they're going to build whole neighborhoods there."

"Uh-huh."

"Take the petroglyph park on the West Side," she said. "The lava-covered land over by the volcanoes is pretty worthless *except* for the petroglyphs. The ancient Native Americans didn't anticipate centuries ago that the pictures they were tapping into the rocks would one day increase the real estate value."

I snorted.

"Everyone knew the feds wanted to turn that whole area of the West Mesa into a national park to protect those hundreds of petroglyphs. Everyone agreed they were worth saving. Good use of our tax dollars, right?"

"Sure," I said. "I kinda remember when it was in the news--"

"Private developers owned much of the land around the future park. When the feds came sniffing around, the value of the land suddenly shot up."

"That's no surprise. People always want to make the most they can--"

"Not this time," she said. "The feds only had so much money to play with, and they didn't want to hand it over to developers. So they said never mind, we can afford to wait. Everything went on hold."

She nodded to herself, like everything she'd said was absolute fact. I could see a few holes and suppositions there, but I didn't say so.

"So what happened?"

"Years went by," she said. "The park plans languished until the developers decided to force the issue. Some of them announced they were going to build big subdivisions on their portions of that land. Even if the park eventually got fully designated, it would be tightly surrounded by houses, blocking the views."

"That's like blackmail. Sort of."

"It worked, too. The feds suddenly resumed negotiations. They went back to the table, and the developers walked away rich."

"I'll be damned," I said. "And this is a pattern?"

"It's happened time and again. And I think it's happening with this latest deal down by the river. The people behind it don't really want to build houses. They're just trying to jack up the price. They produce architectural drawings and street plans for the city Planning Commission, but it's all part of the scam."

"And who pays? The city?"

She cocked an eyebrow at me. "That's why I've been trying to talk to Carlos Martinez."

"Ah."

"He might not be in the middle of it," she admitted. "But if not, then why won't he return my calls?"

I could think of any number of reasons a city councilman would want to avoid Felicia, but I kept them to myself.

"How much money are we talking here?" I said.

"Last time anyone quoted a price for that land, it was six million dollars."

I whistled.

"But the developers say they can turn it into *forty* million if they build houses there instead."

That unpuckered my whistle.

"You could buy a lot of city councilmen for forty million dollars."

"That's what I think, too," she said.

She pointed at her clutter of documents.

"Somewhere in all of that, I'll find the real owners instead of the front men they keep feeding the public. And you can bet we'll find the same old shuck. Nobody wants to actually build Milagro Estates. They just want to pump up the price of that land."

I nodded, like I was considering what she'd said, but there was one touchy subject I wanted to return to. I didn't want to divulge any link to my case, but I had to know.

"Did you say Sammy Vargas was involved? The car dealer guy?"

She gave me a sharp look. "You know him?"

"I just remember those TV commercials. 'Sammy Says Come On Down!'"

I windmilled my arm the way Vargas used to do on camera, waving the viewer into the dealership lot while wearing a big smile.

"Cheesy," she said.

"The cheesiest. Are those still on TV?"

"I don't know. Who has time for TV anymore?"

I was thinking: *It's kinda hard to watch television when the entire living room is covered in papers.*

"Sammy's got no time to make commercials these days," Felicia said. "He's too busy building stuff all over town."

"Yeah?"

"Those apartments going up on Central the other side of Nob Hill? Those are Sammy's. Or, at least, his company is involved in the project. That infill project over on Broadway, where those condos and that hotel are going in?"

"More Sammy?"

She nodded. "Plus a couple of big subdivisions on the West Side. If he keeps going like he has been, people will forget about his beginning in used cars. They'll be putting up statues to Sammy the Builder."

"Hmm." I put on my poker face again. "Any connection between Sammy and Carlos Martinez?"

She squinted at me. "Should there be?"

"I don't know. They're about the same age. I think they both grew up here."

"If there's a connection, I haven't found it yet."

"They probably know each other, at least," I said. "Albuquerque is a small town."

"It used to be. But there are more people all the time. And less vacant land."

"So the price keeps going up?"

That hard glitter returned to her eyes. "Sometimes, the price has help."

"Go get 'em, honey," I said.

"I will."

She smiled, watching as I cleared the table.

"And you?" she said. "Where are you going next?"

"Oh, um, I'm gonna do more interviews. Try to figure out who blabbed about the game."

"You still think that's what happened?"

"I don't have a better theory."

I got out of there before she could ask me any more questions.

Chapter 12

I was behind the wheel of my ancient Oldsmobile, navigating Central Avenue near the University of New Mexico, when my phone tinkled.

I'd set the ringtone to a different song the night before. Jazz piano instead of death metal. Harder to hear, but easier to listen to. I fished my phone out of my pocket and checked the screen. A local number, but I didn't recognize it.

"Hello?"

"Bubba Mabry?"

"Yes?"

"Do you know who this is?"

"I can't say that I do."

"You've been leaving me messages."

"I've left a lot of messages today--"

"To a car dealership?"

Ah. Sammy Vargas. He clearly didn't want me saying his name over the phone. The thought that someone could be listening in made me suddenly anxious. What else shouldn't I say?

I hooked a right turn into the UNM campus and parked the Olds in an asphalt lot overlooking the grassy expanse of Johnson Field. I needed to give the phone call my full attention, and I couldn't do that while running over joggers.

"Yes, sir," I said. "I know which messages you mean. Is it possible that we could talk in person?"

"That's not such a good idea. Just tell me what you want."

"Over the phone?"

"You got a better idea? Can you read my mind from there?"

"All right," I said, trying to keep the annoyance out of my voice. "Think back to last weekend. You got a call, telling you the location of the poker game?"

"Yes. On Saturday afternoon."

"Anyone else hear this call? Your wife? An employee?"

"No."

"Did you mention it to anyone else between the time you got that call and the time you arrived at the game?"

"No."

"That was a pretty quick answer. Are you sure?"

"Absolutely."

I waited.

"I was with my family all day Sunday," he said. "My wife knows I play cards every week, of course, but she never asks about the location or who else is at the table. I had no reason to discuss the game with anyone else."

He sounded certain.

"Any chance someone followed you to the game?"

Vargas at least paused to consider his answer, but it still came back a "no."

"How can you be sure? Were you watching your mirrors the whole time?"

"I didn't go straight to the poker game. I ran a couple of errands late Sunday afternoon, then I went miles out of my way, over to the West Side, to pick up Carlos and give him a ride to the game. I would've noticed someone following me through all that."

"Why did he ride with you?"

Vargas chuckled. "I was test-driving a new Jaguar from one of my dealerships."

"Ah. He didn't mention to me that he'd ridden to the game with you."

"He probably thought it didn't matter," Vargas said. "Frankly, none of this matters. Asking us questions isn't going to get you anywhere. Everyone in that poker game knows that it's strictly private."

"Yet somehow the robbers knew about Sunday's game at the vacant house."

"Shouldn't you be more concerned with what happened *next*? Doesn't it matter more where they went *after* they took our stuff?"

"One thing could lead to the other."

"Hmm."

I felt I had to defend my hypothesis. "If we knew where the leak occurred, I could trace it to the robbers."

"You think so?"

"Maybe."

"Well, good luck with that," Vargas said. "But you won't get any help from me. I'm not the leak, and I don't have any idea who it might be."

No room for argument there, so I said, "Okay."

"Okay."

"But you understand about due diligence," I said. "I have to talk to each of you or I'm not doing my job."

"Fine. We've talked. Anything else?"

"I guess not."

"Listen, friend." His voice softened. "It's real important that you do this quietly. I've got a couple of business deals brewing right now, and I can't afford any bad publicity."

It was all I could do not to mention the land deal that Felicia was studying. A private eye has to be careful about crowing over such knowledge. What you say can and will be used against you.

"I'm being really careful to keep it quiet."

"Aren't you married to a newspaper reporter?"

Ouch.

"I haven't mentioned any of this to her. My investigations are strictly confidential."

He grunted, like he didn't believe me, but he didn't argue.

"I need to go," he said. "I've tied this phone up long enough."

I didn't ask him whose phone he was using, but I did say, "You haven't replaced yours yet?"

"One of my people is taking care of it," Vargas said. "I'm more concerned about the Rolex I lost."

"Was it real valuable?"

"It's worth ten thousand dollars, but it's more about the sentimental value. It was a gift from my wife."

The idea that a wristwatch could be worth ten grand was enough to make me grind my teeth, but I said, "I'll do my best to get it back for you."

"You do that."

Without further ado, he hung up.

Chapter 13

I spent the afternoon driving around with the air conditioner going. I worked my phone, calling sources, following up. Getting nowhere.

I talked to a harried receptionist at Tom Donovan's bank, who assured me she had given him my previous three messages. Mostly, though, I left voicemails. Nobody answers their phone these days. I blame Caller ID. You can't sneak up on anybody by phone anymore. And it's easier to ignore an incoming call than to hang up on somebody who's already said, "Hello."

I'd been lulled into expecting a recording, so I was a little startled when a real human said, "Red's Pool Hall."

"Um. Is this Red?"

"Who else would be answering my phone?"

"Right. This is Bubba Mabry."

"I know."

"What?"

"It says so right here. I've got Caller ID."

"And you answered it anyway?"

"Don't make me regret it."

"Just following up on my earlier visit. You hearing anything about that robbery I mentioned?"

"Not a word," Red said. "That crew must be from out of town or something."

"Huh. That's too bad. I was hoping--"

Somebody loudly honked, alerting me that I was sitting still at a green light. On Lomas Boulevard. At rush hour. I hit the gas and checked the mirror. A jacked-up black pickup truck rumbled behind me. The bearded driver was very red in the face. Some people are so impatient.

Meanwhile, Red said, "A couple of guys came by here today, asking about you."

"Say what?"

"Two guys stopped by the pool hall," Red said. "What, two hours ago? They asked about you."

"Me? What did they want to know?"

"They seemed to know that you'd come by," he said. "They wanted to know what you talked about while you were here. If you were putting out feelers, you know, looking for information."

"What did you tell them?"

"Not a goddamned thing," Red said. "Company policy. We don't talk to cops."

"They were *cops*?"

"They didn't show badges or anything, but they had the mustaches and the sunglasses. They smelled like cops to me."

"Jesus."

I stopped behind other cars at the next red light. The red-faced guy behind me was flipping me the bird, but I ignored him. These sorts of traffic encounters used to rile me, but now that I'm older, I find them easier to disregard. Is that wisdom? Maturity? Or is it simply the increased likelihood that the aggrieved motorist could kick the shit out of a middle-aged guy like me?

"The cops were very casual about it," Red said. "Acting like they were friends of yours. But I know that routine. I told them it had been months since I saw you last."

"Did they believe that?"

"Not for a second. Like I said, they *knew* you'd been by here. Think somebody's following you?"

That made me glance at the rear-view. The red-faced guy was still huffing and puffing in the pickup, but I didn't see anyone else back there who seemed interested in my Oldsmobile.

"I guess it's possible," I said. "But I haven't noticed a tail. Maybe the cops are watching your place?"

A pause.

"I don't have any reason for them to be watching me."

"Maybe they're following one of your customers," I said, "and just happened to spot me while I was there."

"Maybe," he said. "But listen, don't stop by for a while. Just in case it's you they're trailing. I don't need the headache."

"Sure. Call me if you hear anything, okay?"

"Will do."

The phone beeped, showing that Red had hung up. Which was just as well. The light had turned green, and I didn't want to draw another honk.

I slipped the phone into my shirt pocket and sped up, finding a break in the traffic where I could move into the slow lane. The pickup truck rumbled past. Then we all stopped for the next red light.

I didn't even bother looking over at the truck. I had other things on my mind.

Cops? Asking questions about *me* at Red's Pool Hall? What could that *mean*? I didn't have any current cases that should attract the attention of the police, except for the poker-game robbery. I remembered what Gary had said about Goatface's phone and how it would be valuable to the police. Is that why they were asking after me now? Were we hunting the same phone?

I thought about my own phone, the new one. Were the police somehow tracing my movements through my phone? Is that how they knew I'd stopped by Red's Pool Hall? I made a mental note to ask Felicia. She knew more about cell phones than I did. Maybe there was some locator app she could turn off.

The tall truck roared away when the light changed. I checked my mirrors again, but I didn't see anyone who seemed to be following me.

Lomas climbs a long hill as it passes under Interstate 25, and the traffic spread out and sped up as half the vehicles opted for freeway ramps. I stayed in the slow lane, watching my mirrors, letting other cars pass me by.

By the time I reached University Hospital, which looms over Lomas like a great gray battleship, it was apparent that I was in the clear. Still, I drove several extra blocks through my neighborhood, circling around, before I pulled into our empty driveway. I never saw a tail, but my address was no secret. If the cops wanted me, my house would be the first place they'd look.

I felt jumpy as I unlocked the front door, but the neighborhood was as quiet as ever. No sign of Felicia, either. Which was just as well. I needed a few minutes' peace.

And a beer.

Chapter 14

Felicia's mysterious documents had vanished from the living room, so I was able to flop onto the sofa in my usual place. I slugged down a third of my beer and immediately felt better. Goatface's questions about sobriety danced through my head, but I pushed the thoughts away. I was off duty. How I quenched my thirst was none of his business.

Another long swallow, but this one didn't taste as good. And it made me burp, so I got to taste it again. Hmm.

Goatface Odell might be a teetotaler, but he was guilty of plenty of other sins. His underground businesses were part of the reason Albuquerque leads the nation in property crimes every year. You name it, some meth-head is willing to steal it – cars, clothes, cosmetics, catalytic converters, copper wire, power tools, the landscaping right out of your yard. People like Goatface make sure the thieves have a market for their stolen goods.

The thieves risk arrest or worse, but Goatface remained untouchable, protected by lawyers and insulated by layers of paperwork. Even when prosecutors could prove Goatface owned a property where illegal activity was occurring, they couldn't prove he knew what was happening there. All they could hope to accomplish was to make him waste his ill-gotten gains on attorneys' fees.

I figured the other guys around that poker table were equally untouchable. They could make their backroom deals and bank the profits, bold as you please.

The police don't even bother to investigate crime at that level. Why waste resources on white-collar cases they have no chance to win? Better to arrest street-level thieves and junkies. Pump up the crime stats. Fill up the jails. Show the public that crime is everywhere and getting worse and the only answer is more funding for the police.

Meanwhile, the fat cats smirk in their skyscrapers, looking down on the rest of us like they're nobility watching a play. Tragedy looks like comedy from the penthouse. The rich guys pass millions back and forth, laughing all the way to the bank, while the rest of us strive to survive.

Society is a pyramid, mostly based on money and who has it. The wealthy are at the top, and their riches mean they can buy their way out of life's annoyances, up to and including felony charges. Less money means more problems and fewer ways to solve them. So we work our way down the pyramid, through ever greater levels of economic misery, until we get to the bottom, the criminal element, who usually suffer from some combination of poverty and substance abuse and stupidity that keeps them from holding regular jobs.

People at the bottom can't afford to be particular about their morals. They steal what they can, get away with it as long as they can, then turn on their friends when they get caught. Not so different from the fat cats. But which ones go to prison?

I sucked down the last of my beer and was getting up to get another when I heard footsteps on the front porch. Felicia came steaming through the door.

"Hi, honey," I said. "You're home."

Felicia frowned, like I'd stepped on her line.

"Long day," she said. "Beer me."

"On it," I said.

She fell onto the sofa with a sigh while I fetched the Heinekens. I settled onto the cushion next to her and handed her one of the green bottles. I raised mine in a toast.

"To another successful day."

Felicia grunted. "Not so much for me."

"No? Here we are at home. Still breathing. Not in the hospital. Not in jail. To me, that's a successful day."

She cocked an eyebrow at me.

"Did you say 'jail?'"

"Just a hypothetical. I heard some cops were asking around about me today."

"Because?"

"Unclear. But in my line of work, a night in jail is pretty much always a possibility."

"I'll bail you out, hon."

"You've done it before."

We clinked bottles and drank.

"I was thinking before you got here," I said, "about how rich folks don't have to worry about jail and cops and bail. They commit crimes all the time, in search of easy money. But they've got lawyers on the payroll and they play golf with judges on the weekends and they're never held to account."

"Big fish eat little fish," she said. "And they usually get away with it."

She sounded weary. Like she'd been chasing sharks all day.

"If you're rich," I said, "you never spend a day in jail, even if you're clearly guilty. If you're poor, you've got to make bail somehow or you're stuck. If you're stuck in jail, you lose your job because you don't show up. Then you can't support your family, so you're likely to lose them, too. Your whole world falls apart, and you haven't even been convicted of anything yet."

Felicia sighed.

"Are you just now snapping to the inequities built into the American judicial system?"

"You don't have to get all snarky—"

"Are you really that naive?"

"I was just reminded of it because of this poker game situation. Buncha big shots sitting around a table, playing cards, their pockets full of taxpayer dollars. I'm sure they're guilty of all sorts of things, but nobody's investigating them. It's just business."

"And politics," she said.

"One and the same."

That eyebrow again.

"Sounds like you've been reading my stories in the *Gazette*."

I grinned.

"Okay, *you're* investigating them. But the authorities look the other way."

"This good old boy network you're talking about?" she said. "That's who is stonewalling me right now. That's why I can't get any traction on this land deal. Everywhere I turn, people go mum. Documents disappear. Tax records get 'misplaced.' It's exhausting."

We drank in silence for a minute.

"What are you going to do about it?" I asked finally.

"Keep dogging them. Keep sifting through the documents that I can get hold of. Something will break open eventually."

"Atta girl. Where did all your papers go anyway?"

"I commandeered a conference room at the office. It's got a long table where I could spread everything out. I'll head back down there, soon as I get something to eat."

"Sheesh. You never stop working."

"What about you? Any closer to finding your robbers?"

"Not really. I've talked to nearly everybody who was at that game, and they all say the location was kept secret."

"Do you believe them?"

"I can't be sure. I'm not allowed to follow up properly. These rich guys are big into 'because I said so.'"

"They're used to people obeying their orders. That's what wealth buys you."

I thought again about how nobody had specified how I might be getting paid for my time on this investigation. Goatface had ordered me to pursue it, and I had meekly obeyed, without any discussion of my fees. I didn't mention that part to Felicia.

"Where did you go?" she said.

"I was thinking about what you always say: 'Eat the rich.'"

She sucked down the last of her beer and wiped her mouth with the back of her hand.

"The rich are different from you and me," she said. "They're more fattening."

Chapter 15

I was awakened Wednesday morning by the piano stylings of my phone's ringtone. I checked the readout and saw the call was coming from "First State Bank."

The bedroom was full of sunshine. The other side of the bed was empty, only rumpled covers to show that Felicia had once been there. I shook my head to clear the cobwebs, then punched the button to answer the phone.

"Hullo, this is Bubba."

"Good morning. Do you know who this is?"

The deliberate baritone belonged to Tom Donovan, the bank president. It was the grave voice of a man accustomed to giving people bad news.

"Yeah," I said groggily. "I recognize the number."

Which wasn't exactly right, since the phone had recognized it for me, but close enough.

"Good," he said. "That will save a lot of backing and forthing about saying people's full names over the phone. I've got some information for you, and I'd like to keep it brief."

I sat up in a pile of bedclothes, looking around for something to write on and something to write with, but Donovan wasn't waiting.

"I've talked to the other players in the card game," he said.

"Is that so?" I said, checking the drawer of my bedside table for a pen and not finding one.

"Oh, yes." He allowed himself a small chuckle. "I daresay we've been burning up the phone lines, talking about you."

"What's everybody saying?"

"Have you heard the expression 'bull in a china shop?'"

"Sure."

"I'm afraid you're the bull."

"Lots of broken plates, huh?"

"The people in that poker game occupy certain positions in this city," Donovan said. "They're not accustomed to people asking questions. They're used to people saying, 'yes, sir.'"

"Yes, sir."

"They're certainly not accustomed to having private detectives show up at their offices or, worse yet, their courtroom. Your very presence raises questions everywhere you go."

"I can't help what other people--"

"I assure you, when Burt ordered you to do your little investigation, none of us thought it would mean you and your wife would be poking around in our lives."

"My wife has nothing to do with this."

"So you say. Yet she's been calling some of the same people as you."

"It's a coincidence. She was already--"

"You represent a risk, an exposure. None of us wants that."

"So I'm fired?"

"Not at all. Just don't talk to your wife about us. And don't pester the poker players. Keep your distance. If you've got questions for us, funnel them through Gary."

"Okay. But who's my client here? I need to get paid for my time. I was hired for one night--"

"We'll settle up with you when you're done," he said, and I noted that could be taken two ways. "Certainly, we'd insist that you keep any cash that you recovered. Especially if you could return our personal items."

"Like your phones?"

"It doesn't get much more personal than that."

The money taken in that poker game was more than I'd make on a typical investigation. Assuming I could somehow get the loot back from the robbers. Assuming they hadn't spent it already.

"All right," I said. "I'll keep working on it. And I'll communicate with the rest of you through Gary."

"Perfect."

"Does that mean your friend Burt will stop calling me up and demanding results?"

Donovan chuckled, as if the very concept of reining in Goatface was amusing as hell.

"Nobody tells Burt what to do," he said.

"Not even his friends?"

"Not if they want to stay friends."

"Sounds like a hard man to get along with."

"Cross him and you'll find out."

Chapter 16

Naturally, I was annoyed. These big shots. Find the thieves, they say, but don't ask *us* any questions or inconvenience *us* in any way. It's like they asked me to solve a plumbing leak in their home, then locked all the doors so I couldn't come in.

By the time I steamed through my second cup of coffee, I'd thought of one door that remained open. Donovan had said I shouldn't communicate with the men around that poker table, but he hadn't said anything about the dealer.

I had an address for Roz Tate from when I was doing my internet research. I decided that would be my first stop of the day.

I took a shower and shaved, spending way too long in front of the mirror, examining the yellowing bruise on my forehead and the ever-deepening lines on my face. The aging process is a terrible thing to watch, especially in a mirror.

I dressed in khakis and sneakers and a loose white linen shirt, ready for another arid September day in the low 90s. I ate some toast and took some aspirin for the mild hangover nibbling at the edges of my brain. Drank some more coffee. Put on my Isotopes cap to hide my lump.

By the time I got out the door, it was the crack of ten o'clock, and it took twenty minutes to drive up to the Heights and find the Tate home.

It was on a quiet street in a neighborhood where all the stucco houses looked alike – three-car garages facing the street, living quarters in the rear, gravel yards decorated with widely scattered yuccas. Such uniformity always makes me wonder how the drunks find their way home at night.

I parked at the curb next to a cluster of campaign signs and walked across an acre of concrete driveway to reach the front door. Thumbed the doorbell, then waited a full minute before the door was opened by Roz Tate.

"Oh, it's you," she said flatly.

Just once, I'd like somebody to be happy to see me.

"Got a minute?" I said. "I have a few questions."

She leaned out the doorway, looking around, like she was making sure I was alone. Or maybe she was worried about the neighbors watching.

"Come in," she said. "But we'll need to make it quick. I've got a hair appointment in half an hour."

"Near here?"

"Not too far."

I followed her into the living room, which was furnished in a cozy style with plump chairs and lots of pillows and houseplants. Sunlight streamed down from high windows, splashing onto the tile floor.

"Want coffee?" she asked.

"I've had more than enough already. But thanks."

We sat in opposing armchairs. Roz was dressed the same as she had been at the poker game – white blouse and black slacks – but her feet were bare. She curled up in the chair, tucking her feet under her.

"How's your head?"

I lifted the cap so she could see the lump on my forehead.

"Ouch," she said.

"It's not as bad as it looks."

I put my cap back in place and looked around the comfy room.

"Your husband's still in Tulsa?"

"He's flying back this evening. I'm sure he'll want to talk to you about what happened."

"That would be a switch. Nobody else wants to talk to me."

"You mean the poker players?"

"I went to see some of them, and they got bent out of shape. Now, I have to do all my communicating with them through Gary Pierce."

She looked me over.

"Yet here you are," she said.

"A loophole," I admitted. "Nobody said I couldn't question you."

"I don't see how it will do you any good, but ask away."

I wished now that I'd taken the cup of coffee she'd offered. It would've given me something to do while I got my questions ordered in my brain.

"First, I've got to say, I admire how cool you were during the robbery," I said. "You didn't twitch, other than to do exactly what they told you to do."

Her face creased into a little smile.

"I was petrified, if you want to know the truth."

"It didn't show."

"I've been sitting at poker tables for the past twenty years, Mr. Mabry. My face is well-trained to show no emotion. I can't have my eyes lighting up when I see a winning hand. I can't show any sympathy when somebody comes up empty."

I nodded. That made sense.

"But I truly was scared the other night," she said. "I've never looked down a gun barrel before."

"It's happened to me more times than I'd care to admit," I said. "It never gets any easier."

Her blue eyes widened for a second, then her face settled back into its usual repose as she awaited my next question.

"Gary said you were the first to arrive at the game, after him."

She nodded.

"Any chance someone followed you there?"

"There's always a chance, I suppose. But I didn't notice anyone. And that's a pretty quiet neighborhood on a Sunday evening."

"Did you tell anyone you were going to that vacant house?"

She shook her head.

"Not even with your husband out of town? You didn't have a friend standing by in case of emergency, something like that?"

"I've known the men around that poker table for years," Roz said. "I consider them my friends. If I had a flat tire or something, I could count on them to help."

"But you didn't mention that address to anyone? You're sure?"

"Absolutely positive."

"That's what everyone says," I said. "And yet somehow those gunmen knew to stick up that poker game there."

She looked away for a moment, thinking it over. When her gaze returned to me, she said, "You talked to Gary about it?"

"Yeah."

"Did he say anything about setting up the refreshments?"

"Just that he went there early to do that."

"All by himself?"

I hesitated. "Did you see someone else?"

"No, but I got the sense someone had just left. There was a hint of perfume in the air. Gary's hair was mussed. And his Hawaiian shirt was buttoned up wrong. He made a joke about how he must've gone around like that all day."

"Wow."

"And the way that food was so carefully arranged? You think a frat boy like Gary would've been so artistic? I think that shows a feminine touch."

I nodded appreciatively.

"Good details," I said. "You could be a private investigator yourself. You notice things."

That made her smile.

"I've been studying people over card tables my whole life," she said. "Most people are full of 'tells.' If you watch, they'll reveal all sorts of things about themselves."

"Like the secrets they're keeping," I said.

She tilted her head, but said nothing, like she was waiting for me to put it all together myself.

"I thought Gary was a happily married man."

"Maybe he is," she said. "Maybe I'm all wet. Maybe he had a caterer stop by that house and set up the food, and just forgot to mention it."

"A caterer would have no reason to unbutton the client's shirt."

She shrugged.

"Maybe they had a moment. An empty house. Just the two of them. Maybe they got carried away, and he's embarrassed to admit it."

Somehow, that sounded like Gary, the smooth talker. I wondered if he regularly banged clients in vacant houses.

"I talked to him yesterday," I said, "but he didn't mention any of this. I guess I need to interview him again."

"Good idea."

She sounded distracted, and I realized she was looking at a clock that ticked on the wall behind me.

"I've got to go," she said. "I'm going to be late to my hair appointment."

"Right." I jumped to my feet. "You've been a big help. I really appreciate it."

She stood, too, and pointed at my shirt pocket.

"Give me your phone."

"What?"

"Jack will want your number."

I tried to think of some reason to object, but I came up with nothing. I woke up the phone and handed it over.

She dialed quickly, and a phone rang in the next room.

"That's mine," she said. "I'll put your number in my contacts list."

"Okay."

She gave me back my phone. I checked it over for a second, but everything seemed in order. I put it in my pocket.

"Jack will probably call you tonight," she said, "after I pick him up at the airport. He told me he was eager to talk to you. He feels like his security operation has been tainted. He's unhappy about that."

"I'm not happy about it, either. I really wish I hadn't agreed to be his stand-in."

She opened the door for me to leave. A gust of warm wind whooshed inside.

"It's so odd," I said, "that the poker game got robbed the one night when Jack wasn't there. Any possibility someone could've arranged it that way?"

She pushed back her tousled blond hair.

"You think somebody bumped off his elderly aunt in Tulsa?"

"Seems unlikely," I admitted.

"It was a coincidence," she said.

"Those always make me uneasy."

"Yet they happen all the time. They're part of life."

What could I say? She was right.

"Good-bye, Mr. Mabry. Jack will be in touch."

She closed the door.

Chapter 17

Gary Pierce's real estate office was in Nob Hill, one of three offices tucked into the back of a 1950s building that was mostly given over to a yuppie beer joint called Yet Another Brewpub. The office was on the Silver Avenue side of the brick building, a block uphill from busy Central Avenue.

Nob Hill is a trendy shopping-and-dining district just east of the University of New Mexico. During the day, the mile-long stretch of Central Avenue teems with shoppers strolling the sidewalks and visiting funky little stores in old Art Deco buildings. At night, it's alive with foot traffic from the cafes and bars that anchor every block. Walk around Nob Hill on a bustling weekend, and you can feel like you're in a big city.

Pretty quiet on a Wednesday morning, though. I found a parking spot half a block from Gary's office. I fed the parking meter a quarter, which bought me only fifteen minutes, then hoofed it along Silver. The morning sunshine was blinding, even with my sunglasses on, and it was a relief to get indoors.

The real estate office had tinted windows down one side and a solid wall down the other. The wall, painted pale yellow like the rest of the sunny interior, was decorated with two dozen framed photographs of houses currently available for sale. Something about the display made me sad. I realized it reminded me of photos of forlorn pets up for adoption.

I could see Gary behind his desk at the far end of the office. He had his own glassed-in space tucked into the corner. The open middle area held four desks, three of which were occupied by women I took to be real estate agents. They had that polished look about them – hose and heels and hairspray. The youngest one, a thirty-ish woman with thick, dark hair that fell past her shoulders, was downright beautiful. She didn't even look up from her computer as I stepped inside and whipped off my sunglasses.

A desk near the entrance was occupied by a jowly old receptionist who wore a wig that looked like a copper helmet.

"Can I help you with something?" she growled.

I mumbled something about seeing Gary for a minute.

"Do you have an appointment?"

"No, but I can see that he's here." I waved at Gary, who had noticed me at the front desk. He waved back.

"You need an appointment," she said.

"Look, he's right there. I only need a minute."

"We have a schedule to follow around here."

"He's waving at me! Turn around and look. He's gesturing for me to come there."

Which he was. But the old bat wouldn't turn around to look.

The phone buzzed on her desk.

"Don't move," she said to me.

She picked up the receiver and said, "Yes?"

I looked at Gary, exasperated, and could see he was on the phone, too. I assumed he was telling the receptionist to lower the drawbridge.

"Very well," she said into the phone, but her tone said, "You'll be sorry."

She hung up the phone, none too gently, and looked up at me, scowling.

"You can go on back," she said.

"Thanks!" I said brightly. "I'll make an appointment next time."

She gave me a look like there wouldn't be a "next time" if I didn't move it.

The beauty with the long hair giggled as I went past, but I didn't look over at her. I was focused on my mission.

Gary met me at the door of his inner office and gestured me into a chair. My back was to the rest of the room, which was probably was just as well. Last thing I needed was to worry about an office full of lip-readers.

I waited until he'd closed the door before I said, "That's quite a Welcome Wagon you got out there."

"Zelda," Gary said with a sigh. "She doesn't like new faces."

"And she's a receptionist?"

Gary shrugged. "She's been with the firm forever. I think she came with the building."

"That explains the barnacles."

Gary swiveled in his desk chair. He looked tired.

"Did you *want* something, Bubba? Or did you just come by to criticize the office staff?"

I shifted in my chair while I thought about the best way to say it.

"I was talking to Roz Tate," I began.

"When?"

"Just now."

"And?"

"She had the impression that someone was at the house with you, just before she arrived."

Gary tried to maintain his poker face, but his cheeks flushed. Some reactions you can't control.

"You mean when I was setting up?"

"Did you have a caterer helping you? Or maybe someone from here in the office?"

His eyes glanced past me, over my shoulder, then came right back to me. It was only a second, but it was a "tell."

"That beautiful young woman out there? The one with the long hair?"

The flush deepened and crawled up his forehead.

"*She* was at that house?"

Gary gave me a shushing look. I guess I'd gotten a little loud. He leaned across his desk and kept his voice low as he said, "She didn't know anything about the poker game. Until she saw the poker table, she thought it was a private showing for some rich people. Which, in a way, it was. I was hoping one of them would like the house enough to recommend it to a relative or a friend--"

"You didn't mention this yesterday," I said. "You said you were alone there."

"Hold on a second."

He looked over my shoulder again and put on a big smile. Through his teeth, he said, "Don't turn around."

I didn't like the sound of that, but I obeyed. I felt like a sitting duck, behind glass, wondering what the hell was going on behind me.

The smile dropped off Gary's face and he let out his breath.

"Okay," he said. "She's left for an appointment. It's safer to talk now."

I looked over my shoulder and, sure enough, the lovely woman was gone from her desk. The other two agents were on their phones, their backs to us. Zelda faced the front door, alert for intruders.

"Look," Gary said, "I've been having a little fling with Cassandra. It's not serious or anything, but my wife would be very unhappy if she found out about it."

"I bet."

"I told Cassandra I was hosting an event at that vacant house, and she offered to help with the refreshments. It gave us a legit reason to be alone together--"

"I get it," I said. "A fling. And she left just before Roz got there?"

"Yeah, with like a minute to spare. They almost ran into each other."

"And you were still buttoning up your shirt."

The flush again. No wonder Gary lost money at the weekly card games.

"I didn't mention it before because I was embarrassed," he said. "And it didn't matter anyway. Cassandra couldn't have been the one who tipped the robbers."

"How do you know that?"

"She didn't even know it was a poker game until she got there. And she had no idea who would be sitting around that table."

"She could've let it slip to somebody after she left," I said. "Told a girlfriend about you playing poker. The girlfriend tells a friend and, two hours later, we got robbers bashing open the door."

Gary shook his head.

"I asked her," he said. "She swears she didn't mention the game to anyone. She went home after our little liaison, and didn't see anyone else the rest of the evening."

"Or so she says."

"Why would she lie about it?"

I shrugged. "Maybe she wants to cross you up. Maybe she wants your wife to find out what's going on."

He shook his head.

"Maybe she wants to be Mrs. Gary Pierce."

"The job's already taken," he said. "She knows that. I've got kids and a house and the rest of it. I'm not tossing all that aside. This thing with Cassandra, it's a dalliance."

I thought that was an old-fashioned word for it, but I let it go.

"I probably should interview her myself," I said.

"Trust me. It would be a waste of your time. She doesn't know anything and she didn't do anything. What's going on between her and me is a separate issue."

"And that's why you didn't mention it before."

"Why muddy the waters? Your goal is to find the robbers, not to stomp around in my private life."

I nodded and got to my feet.

"All right, Gary. Anything else I should know? Any other secrets?"

He sat up straighter behind his desk, trying to look serious.

"Nothing else."

"Okay. I'll pursue other avenues."

"I appreciate you understanding, Bubba. It's an odd time in my life, and some things are a little out of control--"

I held up my hands to show I didn't want to hear about his mid-life crisis.

"Don't mention it to the other guys, okay?" Gary said. "They wouldn't understand why I kept it to myself. I've already lost their trust. I don't want to get ousted from the game."

"You could always find another poker game."

"Not of this caliber. You know how much money is sitting around that table?"

"I get that, but--"

"I've got business with some of those guys," he said. "Opportunities. I can't afford any distractions."

I nodded, though I was thinking that Cassandra was a big distraction all by herself.

"I'll be in touch," I said.

As I went through the outer office, I made a point of passing close to Cassandra's work station. A name plate on her desk revealed that her last name was "Lyle," which saved me a computer search later.

I walked faster as I passed Zelda's reception desk, but the old lady was on the phone, and I made it past unscathed.

Chapter 18

I was already close to home, so I decided to stop by our brick bungalow for lunch. I almost kept driving when I saw Felicia's car in the driveway, but I reined in the impulse. What if she saw my car going past? How would I explain that? I parked at the curb in front of the house.

It was hot, even on our shady front porch, but I was greeted by a gust of frigid air when I opened the door. Felicia had the cooler going full blast.

She wasn't in the living room, but once I was a few steps inside, I could see through the archway into the dining room, where she sat at the round table, noshing on a sandwich. She was dressed in a loose white shirt and khakis and sneakers. Just like me. We looked like we were on the same bowling team.

She swallowed and pushed up her glasses, looking me over.

"You should've called," she said. "I would've made you a sandwich, too."

"I didn't know I was going to be here for lunch until just now. I was already in Nob Hill, so it was only a hop and a skip to the house."

"What were you doing in Nob Hill?"

I froze. Why had I mentioned that? I'd opened the door to her asking questions. No way that could end well. Still, no point in lying about something so trivial. Since Felicia usually can see through my lies, I save them for the really important stuff.

"I stopped by Gary Pierce's office," I said as I casually tossed my baseball cap onto the coffee table.

"He's in Nob Hill?"

"On Silver."

"Pricey neighborhood."

"Gary's big into first impressions. He drives a red Corvette."

"Ah. And how goes your investigation?"

"I'm no closer to identifying those holdup men. I just keep splashing around in the clients' private lives and making them mad."

"That sounds like you."

"What about you? Making any progress on your big story?"

"A little."

Felicia had left all the fixings out on the counter, so I put together my own sandwich while she told me about it.

"There's a city Planning Commission meeting this afternoon," she said. "The Milagro Estates proposal is on the agenda. Some of my questions are bound to be answered there."

"Such as?"

"Such as who's really backing this deal, and who really owns that land down by the river. I'm tired of sifting through shell companies."

I nodded, busily opening a jar of mayo.

"Guess who's scheduled to speak to the commission? Last-minute addition to the agenda."

"Who?"

"Sammy Vargas."

I paused in my sandwich-building. The car dealer seemed to be everywhere.

"He's one of the Milagro developers," she said. "But he's not the only one. They've got some heavy hitters lining up on their side. Including that big-deal banker, Tom Donovan."

I jolted in surprise, smearing mayo over the back of my hand.

"Do you know him?"

"Not exactly." I used a paper towel to clean my hands. "We've met."

Silence while I finished putting my turkey sandwich together. With the ruffled lettuce and sliced pickles and other fixings, it was nearly as tall as it was wide. I carried my plate to the table and sat across from Felicia. Her eyes were on me the whole time.

"Is Donovan in that poker game?" she asked as I took a big bite. "Is that how you met him?"

This might've been a good time for one of those important lies, but I wasn't quick enough and I had a mouth full of sandwich. She saw the reaction on my face.

"He *is*! Oh, my God."

I chewed faster. I needed to find a way to derail her.

"Is Vargas in the game, too?"

"I never said--"

"With Carlos Martinez?"

"You're making assumptions--"

"And *Goatface Odell*!"

I clamped my mouth shut. I would neither confirm nor deny.

"These games could be part of the story," she said. "At minimum, the fact that they're all in the same room together violates the state Open Meetings Act. If they discuss city business at all, they could be in big trouble."

"It didn't seem like that kind of game to me. I didn't hear anyone discussing business. They were focused on their cards."

She scoffed.

"You can't tell me those guys gather once a week and never talk about their intersecting business deals."

No, I couldn't tell her that. Because I'd been having the same sort of thoughts about the men around that poker table.

"You know what you've done, Bubba? You've stumbled onto a branch of the good old boy network. The real movers and shakers in this town. I'll bet all kinds of important decisions get made at those poker games."

"Well, it wouldn't be a complete surprise, I guess. People talk when they get together, but--"

"Behind closed doors," Felicia said. "That's always the way of these deals. The important decisions are made in private. The public hearings are just for show."

"Sure, but--"

"It's no coincidence that Vargas and Donovan are involved in Milagro Estates together," she said. "They've probably been planning it for years over those weekly card games."

"Maybe so, hon, but--"

"And it's in Martinez's district! You know he must be tearing off a piece of the profits."

I opened my mouth to mount an argument, but I didn't even get any words out before I was interrupted.

"They're using their phony subdivision to jack up the price, then Martinez will get the City Council to rush the purchase of the land. He'll say they've got to act before the bulldozers ruin that precious riverfront open space."

I didn't even try to respond. She was on a roll. She didn't need me.

"Except there aren't any bulldozers. It's a bluff. The bogus subdivision is leverage, that's all. A way for everyone involved to make more money."

Her eyes were shiny with excitement behind her smudged glasses. I have found that, when she gets like this, it's better to stay out of the way. I focused my attention on my sandwich, waiting for her zeal to die down a little.

"Oh, and who else is in this poker game?" she said. "A *real estate agent.* Just what you need if you're trying to hide your land deal in a flurry of paperwork."

I couldn't let that pass. Gary Pierce was my client, more or less, and I felt a certain loyalty.

"Do you have any indication that Gary was involved in any of this? Is his name on any of the documents or anything?"

"Not that I've seen," she admitted. "But that doesn't mean he's not involved behind the scenes."

She had me there.

"What kind of real estate does he do?"

"Upscale homes, mostly," I said. "That's what they have pictured on the wall at his office."

"Hmm. I'll bet he does commercial work, too."

I shrugged. My sandwich was dwindling, and I could already tell it wasn't going to sit well in my stomach. Too bad. It was starting to look like a busy afternoon ahead.

Felicia apparently was having similar thoughts.

"I've got to go to that Planning Commission meeting," she said. "Vargas and Donovan have been dodging me, but I can pin them down in person, and ask about these card games--"

"No, you can't."

"What?"

"You can't let on that you know they're in the poker game together," I said. "They'll blame me for telling you."

"You didn't tell me," she snarled. "I *surmised* it. All you did was sit there with your big mopey face, giving off signals whenever I mentioned another name."

I wanted to object to this characterization, but it undoubtedly was accurate.

"Guess I don't have a poker face," I said. "Good thing I don't gamble."

"Yeah, good thing. We'd be in the poorhouse by now."

"They don't have those anymore."

"What?"

"Poorhouses."

"It's just an expression, Bubba."

"There used to be actual poorhouses," I said. "If you went broke, you got to go to the poorhouse and work off your debt. Now, in the same situation, you're homeless. Isn't that worse?"

She squinted at me. She used to do that a lot when she smoked cigarettes. I'd always assumed she was squinting against the smoke, but she still does it, years after she kicked the habit. Turns out it's her native skepticism making her squint. No kicking that.

"You're changing the subject," she said, "but don't think I've been distracted. I'm going to that meeting and I'm going to buttonhole Vargas and Donovan--"

"They'll never believe that I didn't tell you. Screw up their deal, and they'll take it out on me."

"What they'll do? Fire you? So what?"

"They can ruin me. Like you said, they're power brokers in this town. If they put out the word against me, I might never work again."

"Forgive me for saying so, Bubba, but most of your clientele isn't in real tight with the power brokers. I doubt they'd notice if you were blackballed."

I took a deep breath. Time to play my trump card.

"What about Goatface? He's been known to disappear people. You said so yourself. If they think I exposed their secret poker game, he might send some of his goons around--"

"Oh, come on. Now you're being melodramatic."

"You just got through saying these big shots can get away with anything. What's to stop them from vanishing me?"

She sighed.

"So what am I supposed to do? Sit through the Planning Commission meeting, pretending everything's fine, while Vargas and Donovan act like they don't know each other?"

"I know it's asking a lot, but--"

"I can't do it," she said. "I can't let them wriggle away again. They're perpetrating a scam on the taxpayers, and I won't let them get away with it."

"Even if it puts me in jeopardy?"

"You can take care of yourself."

Which was maybe the nicest thing Felicia had ever said to me, though we both knew it was largely untrue.

I stood and took my dishes over to the growing stack in the sink. I could stay here and fight with Felicia, or I could get back out into the world and maybe head off a disaster.

I told her I had an appointment, and had to get going. I asked her one more time not to confront Vargas and the rest of them until I was no longer involved.

"If I wait," she said, "it'll be too late. Once the Planning Commission votes, the City Council almost always follows that recommendation. Your poker players are trying to steamroll this deal through. There's no time to lose."

I could see I wasn't going to get anywhere with her. I had to take action on my own.

"I'll see you later then," I said, a little more gruffly than I intended.

I plucked my Isotopes cap off the coffee table and set it on my head, covering my bruised brow. Then I hustled out of there. If I didn't head off this Planning Commission crisis, a bruise would be the least of my problems.

Chapter 19

I needed to tell Sammy Vargas that he was on a collision course with Felicia. And that it wasn't my fault.

I didn't have a phone number for Vargas, and this was a warning better delivered in person anyway. I knew from my internet research that he still worked every day at his original car dealership, the headquarters for his ever-growing empire.

Sunlight bounced off acres of shiny vehicles at the competing auto dealerships that line Lomas near Wyoming Boulevard. I squinted behind my sunglasses, trying to make out the entrance to Vargas' business. I spotted it at the last second and stood on my brakes and whipped a left across three lanes. Someone behind me honked.

I crept up and down the rows of new vehicles until I found a visitors parking area near the building's entrance. I steered my wheezing Olds into a parking slot. I hadn't even gotten the key out of the ignition before a tall, raw-boned guy in a straw cowboy hat appeared at my window, bent over and grinning at me.

"Howdy!" he shouted through the glass. "Welcome!"

He stepped back far enough that I could open my door, but no farther. No room for escape. I squeezed out of the gap and right into a vigorous handshake.

"Ralph T. Ronson," he said, pumping away. "My friends call me Big Ralph. It's a pleasure to meet you."

He paused, waiting for me to take my turn.

I mumbled my name, and he stared at me, smiling and unblinking, still holding onto my paw, until I repeated myself. When it finally got through, he let go of me and clapped his hands together.

"Bubba!" he said. "That's a fine name! I once had a bird dog named Bubba. Are you a hunter, sir? No? I gotta tell you, there's nothing quite like working with a good bird dog out in the field."

He looked into the distance for a moment, a little misty with nostalgia for the innocent birds he'd blasted to kingdom come. Then his attention snapped back to me, all business.

"So what are we looking for today? A new car? A truck? I've got a fresh shipment of pickups, all of them tricked out and ready to roll. You like red? I've got a red truck out on the lot that'll make you weep, it's so beautiful."

He finally had to take a breath, and I jumped on the opportunity.

"Not shopping," I said quickly.

"I understand," he said, just as quickly. "You just want to look. That's what everybody says. But once you see this year's models, you'll--"

"Not interested."

"Absolutely. You don't want some salesman hanging on your elbow while you look. I get that. I'll just hang back, and if you have any questions--"

"Sammy Vargas."

"What's that?"

"I'm here to see Sammy Vargas."

His smile withered and died.

"You know Mr. Vargas?"

I nodded. No need to go into how shallow that acquaintance might be.

"So you're not buying a car today?"

I shook my head. Silent gestures seemed to be the safer way to go. No way for Big Ralph to use my words against me.

"All righty, then," he said. "Guess we're wasting each other's time."

His smile returned and he pointed at the building.

"Go through that door, then take a right. Mr. Vargas' office is at the far end. But of course, you probably already know that, since you and Mr. Vargas are friends and all."

The smile didn't budge, but his eyes went flinty. I thanked him and danced away. He watched me all the way to the door.

Icy air-conditioning greeted me as I went inside, chilling the sweat on my shirt. A dozen people sat at desks in the big open office, and most wore sweaters. Beyond them, a row of glassed-in private offices ran along the wall, terminating in a corner office that allowed Sammy Vargas to look out over his acres of autos.

Naturally, a receptionist stood between Sammy and me. She wasn't a hundred years old like Zelda at Gary Pierce's office, but she was experienced enough not to take any crap from some middle-aged guy dressed in sneakers and a ball cap. She pointed me into a waiting area and told me she'd let Vargas know I was there. Her tone told me not to get my hopes up.

I chose a chair that gave me a view of Sammy's office across the way. He never looked over at me, too busy talking on the phone, and he might not have recognized me anyway, since I was wearing my Isotopes cap.

He was a sleek-looking man, plump and shiny, with a manicured mustache and a sprinkle of silver in his black hair. He wore a Western-style shirt with the sleeves cuffed back on his thick forearms and a chunky gold watch in place of his missing Rolex. A rich guy like Vargas probably had a dozen wristwatches.

He appeared to take one call after another, all the while sifting through papers on his desk. With each passing minute, I felt more ill at ease. What was I doing here? I didn't owe Sammy Vargas anything. To warn him away from the Planning Commission meeting would be a betrayal of Felicia, plain and simple. She trusted me when she told me about her investigation of Milagro Estates. And here I was, ready to betray that trust, just to save my own skin.

It was purely happenstance that Felicia's investigation and my one-night gig as security guard ended up colliding, but there was no way I could persuade the poker players of that. They would think I was working with Felicia the whole time. I tried not to imagine the reaction of Goatface Odell, but scenes of violence kept coming to mind.

Suddenly, Vargas jumped to his feet at his desk, his face twisting into a scowl. He looked to be shouting into the phone, though I couldn't hear anything through the wall of glass. He jabbed at the air with his finger, like he was telling off someone who was right in front of him instead over the phone.

His sudden fury unnerved me. Clearly, he was not in a good mood right now. It seemed a bad time to warn him about Felicia and her conspiracy theories.

I watched for a few more seconds while Vargas barked and snarled into the phone. Then he slammed down the receiver. He stood with his hands on his hips, breathing heavily, staring out the window while he calmed himself.

It seemed like a good opportunity to slip away. I scurried out of the waiting area and past the receptionist, who called behind me, "Sir?"

I didn't look back. I kept going, bursting through the front door, out into the bright sunshine.

Big Ralph loitered near the door, waiting for his next victim to pull into the parking lot. When he saw me, he said, "That was quick."

I didn't respond. I hurried along the sidewalk to my Oldsmobile, which sat in full sun, heat waves rising off its metal skin. I climbed behind the wheel, gasping at the oven-like interior, and keyed the ignition. The engine groaned and coughed.

"Not now," I said through gritted teeth. I tried it again. The engine turned over, but immediately died.

Big Ralph was headed my way, the grin back on his face.

I pumped the gas pedal and turned the key and the engine sputtered to life. I backed away before the salesman could reach me. I zipped past a long line of new cars to reach the exit.

I checked the rear-view, and I could see Big Ralph back there, his hands on his hips, his cowboy hat tipped back on his head. He smiled ruefully, like I was the one who got away. Which was exactly what I intended to do. I caught a break in the traffic on Lomas and got away from there.

Chapter 20

I drove in the slow lane, chewing on my lip, feeling like a coward for not facing Sammy Vargas. But he'd seemed so angry, and I had to assume that anger was somehow connected to me. Everywhere I went, people got pissed off.

I was under orders not to bother Sammy and the other poker players anyway. I was supposed to funnel all contact through Gary Pierce. I should let *Gary* know about Felicia and the Planning Commission meeting. Let him give the others the bad news.

I started looking around for a place to pull over and call him, and that's when I noticed a car shadowing me. A black Ford four-door sedan, the type cops drive. I couldn't see who was inside the car, but it looked like the silhouettes of two men.

I remembered what Red had said about his pool hall being visited by two men who looked like cops. My heart beat faster.

I could barely drive for watching the mirror, but I'm nothing if not impulsive. Without thinking it through, I hit the brakes and swerved onto a side street. I was immediately in a quiet residential area. The houses were modest stucco cubes. Old cars and rusty trucks lined the curbs.

I went a couple of blocks before I reached a stop sign. I checked the mirror. The black Ford had turned onto the street behind me. It hung back, inching along, giving me the creeps.

I stomped the gas, and the Olds shuddered through its gears. I ran the next stop sign, taking a left without signaling. There was no traffic anyway. Just that black Ford swimming in my wake.

The neighborhood was unfamiliar. After twenty years of prowling Albuquerque on various investigations, I thought I knew every corner of the city. But this subdivision had blind curves and dead ends where it pressed up against the concrete canyon that contains Interstate 40.

The Ford was right behind me now. The sun angling through the windows illuminated the two men in the front seat. They were two of a kind, white guys wearing black sunglasses. Short hair and thick necks and matching mustaches.

I took a sudden right, thinking the street would get me back to Lomas. Big mistake. The street ended in a blob of asphalt surrounded by stucco houses. Just beyond the houses loomed the concrete sound-barrier walls that line the freeway.

Cul-de-sac. French for "your nuts are in a trap."

I powered the Olds through a U-turn that made the tires shriek, but it was too late. The black Ford had stopped in the street at an angle, blocking my escape.

Shit.

The doors flew open and the two men got out.

Double shit.

I didn't see any badges and they were dressed in jeans and polo shirts, the plainest of plain clothes, but they had the muscle and menace of cops.

The driver was an inch or two taller than his partner and a few years older, but they looked enough alike to be brothers. The driver came up to my side of the car while his partner went to the passenger side. They peered in through the glass for a second, checking out the interior. Then they nodded at each other. Like they were confirming they'd found the guy they were looking for. Yikes.

The driver twirled his finger in the international symbol for "roll down your window," though windows haven't rolled down that way in generations. I hesitated. He frowned. My finger hit the switch. The window hummed down.

"Get out of the car," he said.

"Wait a minute," I said. "Who are you guys? What do you want?"

"Get out."

"Why are you following me?"

"Get out of the car."

"I know my rights. You can't just order me around."

He sighed, exasperated. Then he reached through the open window and unlocked my door and popped it open before I even realized what was happening.

"Get out."

I got out.

He slammed the door, which left us standing too close to each other, my sweaty back pressed against the Olds. His partner came around the rear of the car, closing in, so I had no room to move.

"Bubba Mabry," the driver said, his mouth twisted into a sneer.

"That's right," I said. "And you would be?"

"I'm your worst nightmare."

"Actually, my worst nightmare is the one where I show up to take a test in school and I'm not wearing any clothes. And the teacher is a walrus--"

He poked me in the chest with his stiff index finger.

"Ouch."

"Don't talk," he said. "Just listen."

I pressed my lips together to keep any more sass from spilling out.

"You've been asking around about a stickup at a poker game."

I shook my head, but even silent denials weren't any good with this guy. He poked me in the chest again. Harder.

"You're gonna stop doing that now," he said. "Stop asking questions. Stop bothering people. Understand?"

I hesitated.

Poke.

"Okay, okay. I'll stop asking questions. But at least tell me who you're working for. That way, I'll know which toes I'm stepping on."

The driver looked over at his partner.

"Was that a question?"

The partner shrugged.

The driver looked back to me. "Didn't I say no more questions?"

"It wasn't a question, exactly--"

He slapped the hat off my head.

"Hey, now. There's no need to--"

He poked me again, this time right on the bruise in the center of my forehead. That really hurt, and I clapped both my hands to my face.

I felt a tug on the front of my shirt. When I blinked my eyes open, I saw that his partner had plucked my new phone from my shirt pocket. He punched at the screen, but didn't seem to get anywhere. He looked up at me.

"Did you call anybody while we were driving around?"

"No, but you have no right to--"

Poke. Right on the bruised lump again. The driver had unerring aim, I'll give him that. My hands went to my face again.

I opened my eyes just in time to see the partner throw my phone down on the pavement. It cracked.

"Aw, man," I said. "That was brand-new--"

The driver stomped on my phone for good measure. The screen broke into bits under his black sneaker.

Then they turned away from me, all done for now. They strutted back to the Ford, gloating, sharing a high five on the way.

I didn't move until they'd driven out of sight.

Chapter 21

I stooped to pick up my cap. I dusted it off and gently set it on my head. My forehead throbbed.

I looked around at the nearby houses, but nobody seemed to be watching out the windows. Everybody at work this time of day. Given the lack of witnesses, I was probably lucky the Mustache Brothers hadn't hurt me worse.

I gathered up the larger pieces of my shattered phone and put them in my pocket. No putting it back together, but the SIM card probably could be salvaged. I was near the Uptown phone store. I could get another phone, but that could take a while. I needed to get word to Gary Pierce right away, before people started showing up for that Planning Commission meeting.

My first thought was a pay phone, but when was the last time you saw a pay phone? They're gone. If your own phone is broken, you're out of luck.

I decided the fastest way to reach Gary would be to simply drive over to his office. It was only five minutes away, depending on traffic.

Naturally, I hit every light red on my way to Nob Hill, which gave me plenty of time to reconsider. I felt bad, potentially screwing up Felicia's scoop, but I just didn't see any other way.

My head throbbed, and I felt overheated whenever I thought of that guy stomping my phone. I turned up the air-conditioning in the Olds. I gently pushed back my cap and checked my forehead in the rear-view. No visible change in the bruise, but it sure did hurt.

Who *were* those guys? Were they cops? If so, why not show badges? Were they *dirty* cops? Who were they working for? Why did they care if I investigated a robbery?

Fortunately, I was stopped for a red light when I finally had this thought: Were the Mustache Brothers two of the *robbers*? I jerked all over at this sudden apprehension, and would've driven right up onto the sidewalk if I'd been moving.

The robbers had been fit white guys about the size of the ones who had just accosted me. No way to be absolutely sure of their identities – they'd worn ski masks to the holdup and sunglasses this time around – but it was possible they were the same guys. The robbers had worn black sneakers, too.

Not a lot to go on, but my mind raced with the possibilities, and I didn't realize the traffic light had changed. Somebody honked behind me. I hit the gas and zoomed along for two blocks before I came to another red light.

As I stewed behind the wheel, I wondered how the Mustache Brothers had known to find me way out on Lomas. Had they been following me the whole day? Were they *still* following me? I twisted around in the seat, checking windows and mirrors, but couldn't see anybody who seemed interested in my car.

I was ready when the traffic light changed this time, but still someone behind me honked before I could get off the brake. Jesus, these people. How is a man supposed to think?

Central Avenue was coming up, and I hooked a right and headed toward Nob Hill. More red lights on Central, but I didn't mind the delay now. I was onto something.

How did those guys in the black Ford even know I was investigating the robbery? How did they know about the poker game? If they were willing to jack me up in broad daylight, they must think I'm getting close to something. I wondered what it could be.

I had to make the block before I found a parking space near the real estate office. I didn't have any change for the parking meter, but I figured I could risk it; I should only be in Gary's office for a few minutes.

As I walked to the entrance, I made a plan for dealing with Zelda the zealous receptionist. She might be tough of tongue, but she didn't look particularly spry. I figured I could outrun her.

I pushed open the door to the real estate office and was welcomed by a blast of air-conditioned cool. I whipped off my sunglasses and gave Zelda a big smile. She glowered at me. Then I hot-footed it right past her.

"Hey!" she croaked.

I veered between desks and hurried all the way to the door of Gary's inner office before Zelda could make it to her feet. The other women in the office watched me go by, but never stopped talking into their phones.

Gary could see me coming through his walls of glass, of course, but I still knocked before I opened his door. Zelda glared at me as I went inside.

Gary looked even worse than when I'd last seen him, as if he'd been recently gut-punched.

"Hey," I said as I closed the office door behind me. "Are you okay? Is this is a bad time?"

"It's a terrible time," he said. "Nobody could make it any worse, not even you."

That smarted, but I let it go.

"What's wrong?"

He opened his mouth, like he was about to spill his problems, but he thought better of it. He swallowed whatever he'd been about to say.

"Nothing that matters to you. Business stuff."

I waited, but he didn't seem willing to volunteer anything more.

"All right," I said. "'Business stuff' is why I'm here. I need you to get word to Sammy Vargas and Tom Donovan. Right away."

"Word about what?"

"There's a Planning Commission meeting this afternoon," I said, "focusing on some land down by the river."

He nodded to show he knew what I was talking about.

"Vargas and Donovan are both supposed to be there," I said.

More impatient nodding. Like I was telling him stuff he already knew.

"So is my wife."

He blinked twice.

"What did you just say?"

I took a deep breath. This was hard enough. It didn't help that I had to spell it out for him.

"My wife, Felicia Quattlebaum, the *Gazette* reporter? She's been digging into Milagro Estates. She thinks there's something fishy about it. Vargas and Donovan have been dodging her."

Gary looked smaller in his chair the longer I talked, like he was deflating.

"She's going to ambush them at that meeting," I said. "I thought you should warn them."

He thought it over for a moment, looking less happy all the time.

"They're used to dealing with the news media," he said. "I'm sure they've got people who will run interference for them."

"You don't know my wife," I said. "When she decides to do something, people tend to get out of the way."

"I hate to throw a scare into everybody. I mean, what can she do but ask questions? Does she have any proof of anything?"

I shrugged.

"I don't know for sure. But I think she figured out their connection to the poker game."

"She *what?*"

"I didn't tell her anything," I said quickly. "But she, um, she *surmised* that there was a connection there."

"She surmised it."

"Yeah."

"Based on what information? Did you tell her about the robbery?"

"A little. I couldn't very well keep the whole thing secret."

I lifted my Isotopes cap and pointed at the lump on my forehead.

"Bruises like this tend to get her attention. So I told her I was at a poker game and I got knocked in the head. But I didn't tell her any names or anything."

"Then how did she figure out that Vargas and Donovan are in the game?"

I shrugged. Sometimes, a gesture is as good as a fib.

Gary sighed.

"The guys are not going to be happy about this. The Planning Commission meeting is a big deal. The timing of it--"

"Maybe they'll decide to go anyway," I said. "But I thought you'd want to let them know she would be there and she might ask questions about the poker game."

Gary rubbed his face with both hands, like he could massage away the worry. I hated to nudge him, but I said, "Donovan said all contact should go through you--"

"I know, I know." He took his hands away and focused on me. "I'll take care of it."

"Right away? That meeting's coming up in--"

"Right away."

I got to my feet. Gary stayed in his swivel chair, watching me.

"Hey," I said. "You know anything about two guys in a black Ford? Sunglasses? Mustaches?"

He shook his head, clearly bewildered.

"They pulled me over a little while ago and roughed me up," I said. "Told me to stop asking questions about the robbery."

"Who were they?"

"I thought they might be cops. They had that air about them. But then I thought, maybe they were the robbers themselves."

That made his eyes go wide.

"Who knows?" I said. "Maybe we'll see them again."

Gary took a deep breath and blew it out.

"Could this situation get any more screwed up?"

"I've got a bad feeling it will get worse before it gets better." I reached for the door. "You've got calls to make. I'll get out of here and let you make them."

Through the glass, I could see that the scowling old receptionist stood next to her desk, her fists on her hips, waiting for me.

"But first," I said to Gary, "can you call off Zelda?"

Chapter 22

When I got back to my car, I found a parking ticket pinned under the windshield wiper. Muttering curses, I snatched the ticket off the car and stuffed it into my pocket.

I felt ragged as I got behind the wheel, and the parking ticket didn't help. I took a few deep breaths, trying to relax. I'd turned the most immediate problem over to Gary. That insulated me from the other poker players, at least for the moment.

Would they believe it was pure coincidence that Felicia's investigation crossed paths with mine? Would they believe I'd done nothing to reveal their secrets to her? Probably not. The bigger question: What would they do about it? Unclear, but I felt sure the situation would find a way to bite me in the ass.

I cranked the starter of the Oldsmobile a few times before the engine caught. That worried me, but the car drove fine through Central Avenue's construction zones and crowded intersections. I took Louisiana Boulevard north to Uptown. The parking lot of the phone store was nearly full. I sighed. I'd hoped for a quick stop here. I had investigating to do.

Inside, I had to take a number and wait for a "customer service representative." My luck being what it is, I drew the same sweaty basement dweller who'd waited on me last time. He still smelled slightly of mildew.

"I remember you," he said. "You were just in here."

I took the largest piece of my broken phone out of my pocket and handed it over.

"Had a little accident," I said. "I'll take the same model again."

"Are you sure? Maybe the universe is telling you it's time to get an upgrade."

"Maybe the universe is telling you to make sturdier phones."

That made him smile. I was serious.

"We'll compromise," he said. "I'll show you the latest in protective cases. Clearly, you're hard on your phone. I've got cases that are like armor."

"Will it still fit in my shirt pocket?"

He rolled his eyes and went off to find me a new phone.

While I waited, I wandered over to the windows and checked the parking lot. No sign of the black Ford. Maybe the Mustache Brothers figured I was no longer a concern now that they'd warned me off the case, but threats rarely work on me. I'm too stubborn.

The salesman returned and unboxed a new phone. I nodded approvingly, then he went through the steps of installing my SIM card and my contacts and my apps. When he finished, he handed the phone over to me.

"Ready to go."

"What about the ringtone?" I asked. "What's it set on?"

His cheeks flushed, but he didn't admit anything.

"Regular factory setting," he said. "But it's easy to set whatever ringtone you like. Want me to show you?'

"I'll figure it out," I said, my point made.

I charged the five-hundred-dollar phone to my business credit card, where the debt was growing with every passing replacement.

Once I was behind the wheel of the Olds, air-conditioner running, I checked the phone's settings. Sure enough, the ringtone was set at the factory default. I switched it over to the jazz piano riff that I'd chosen before, then put the phone away.

Before I could even pull out of my parking space, the phone start playing the piano in my pocket. I checked the readout. Not a number I recognized, but I hit the button to answer.

"Bubba Mabry Investigations."

"You fucking idiot," said a man on the other end of the line. "What have you done?"

Several possible answers there, so I wasn't sure which way to jump.

"What?"

"Like you don't know," he said sarcastically. "This thing at the Planning Commission. What a total cock-up."

I recognized the bleating voice. Burt "Goatface" Odell.

"It wasn't my fault," I said. "Felicia was already onto that land deal long before the poker game."

"Did you know about it before Sunday night?"

"No, sir. I had no idea what she was up to. I rarely do."

"But you told her about the game?"

"Only to explain away the knot on my head. I didn't give her any names or anything."

He scoffed. I said nothing, waiting. If he was going to fire me, this would be the time.

"Some of the same people are involved in both things," he said finally. "But the land development has nothing to do with the poker game. Totally separate."

I didn't believe that, but I said, "All right."

"Focus on finding those robbers," Goatface said. "Get back what they stole. Particularly my phone. I told you before, it's important that I get it back. A lot of my business is tied up with that phone."

"I've got some ideas," I said. "About who those guys might be."

I hoped he didn't ask me to expound upon these ideas because they were thin to mostly cloudy. But I was trying to sound positive.

"I don't want to hear your lame theories," he said. "I want results. Time is running out."

"Yes, sir."

A pause, but he didn't hang up immediately. I took advantage of the opportunity.

"Hey," I said, "you know anything about two guys with mustaches and muscles who drive a black Ford? I caught them following me earlier. They told me I should stop asking questions about the robbery."

"Who were they?" he asked.

"I don't know. I'm asking if you know."

"What are you, stupid?" he snarled. "I'm the one who hired you to find those thieves. Why would I send a couple of goons to tell you to stop?"

He had a good point there.

"Never mind," I said. "I'll call Gary as soon as I know anything."

"Call me directly," he said. "At this number."

I hesitated. "Okay. What about the others?"

"There are no others," Goatface said. "You're working for me. The rest is just noise. Understand?"

"Yes, sir.'

"So stop making noise, and go find my phone."

No pause this time. The call disconnected.

I took a deep breath and blew it out again. Every chat with Goatface felt like a reminder of mortality.

I put the phone in my pocket and it immediately played its piano tune again. What the hell?

I pulled it out and checked the number. Never seen it before.

"Bubba Mabry Investigations."

"Hey," said a gravelly voice. "This is Jack Tate."

The poker dealer's husband. At last.

"Hello there," I said. "Back home from your trip?"

"Yeah. Why don't you come see us? I think you know the address."

"Okay," I said. "When should I stop by?"

"Now's good."

I wanted to object, but the fact was that now was as good a time as any.

"All right," I said. "I'll see you in fifteen minutes."

He grunted an assent into the phone and hung up without saying good-bye.

I gingerly put the phone back in my shirt pocket, fearing it might go off again. Nothing this time.

Jack Tate had not sounded happy, but his wife had said he wasn't known for his cheery disposition. This wasn't a conversation to look forward to, but it beat talking about the Planning Commission meeting.

Chapter 23

Jack Tate was a big-boned man in his early fifties who looked like he still started every day with a hundred push-ups. He was five inches taller than me, and probably outweighed me by fifty pounds. His shoulders were nearly as wide as the doorway as he showed me into the house. He had thick hands with scarred knuckles, and his gray hair retreated from a heavy brow.

No wonder he'd spent all those years as a patrol cop. A guy this size shows up at a fracas, people tend to calm down.

Roz occupied the same armchair as the last time I saw her, feet tucked up under her. She was dressed in jeans and a linen tunic, so I guessed she was off-duty today. Jack wore jeans and white sneakers and a black T-shirt that hugged his muscular frame.

He pointed me into an armchair. He sat on a chair to my left, his elbows on his knees, his big hands knit together. Sort of perched on the edge of his seat, like he might lunge at me any minute. I caught myself wincing in anticipation.

"Roz tells me you're investigating this robbery," he began.

"Not by choice," I said. "I thought I was doing a one-night gig, helping out an occasional client. Instead, it's spiraled into something bigger. Burt Odell insisted that I get involved."

He nodded, like none of that surprised him.

"He thought it was funny, the coincidence?" Jack said.

"Which one?" I thought for a moment he was talking about Felicia's land deal investigation.

He looked puzzled for a moment, then said, "That the thieves hit the game on the one night that I was out of town."

"He didn't specifically mention that, but it did seem a little suspicious, frankly. I asked Roz about it when I was here before."

"Because you suspected me," he said.

"Just covering all the bases."

"What about you?" he said. "Don't you think the others suspect you for the same reason?"

"Sure, I was the new guy in the room--"

"Why do you think Goatface is making you do the investigating? It's his way of fucking with you."

I hadn't considered that possibility. Did Goatface suspect that I was the leak? Did the others? I was the one person I *knew* hadn't revealed the game's location to anyone, but I could see how the poker players might see it differently. They didn't know me. Why should they trust me?

"So how's it going, this investigation of yours?" Jack asked. "You making any progress?"

I looked from him to Roz and back again. They were keeping it friendly, but they had ice in their eyes.

"Not much," I admitted. "Mostly, I've just been stirring things up, making people mad."

He nodded.

"And I had a couple of guys threaten me today, telling me to drop the investigation or bad things will happen."

I told him about the Mustache Brothers in the black Ford. If he knew anything about them, it didn't show on his face.

"I thought they might be police," I said. "They never showed badges, but they sort of worked as a team, you know? Like they'd done this together before."

"That doesn't mean they're police officers. Anybody can do what you described if they've got the balls. And if the person they're accosting is gullible enough to assume that they're law enforcement."

I didn't like this defensiveness, but it's what I expected. Cops, even retired cops, always stick together.

"It also occurred to me," I said, "that they could've been two of the robbers. They were the right size and they wore black sneakers like the guys on Sunday night."

Jack scoffed.

"Whoever they are," I said, "they somehow found out I was asking around about the robbery and decided to make me stop."

"Seems to me it would be safer to ignore you. They've been successfully lying low. Why would they suddenly brace you?"

"I don't know. They've been complete professionals. The way they handled the robbery with those shotguns, the way they used a battering ram on the door. Quick and efficient. Another reason I thought they might be police."

"Again, that doesn't really mean anything," he said. "Anybody can plan a quick robbery. And it's not illegal to possess a battering ram. You can buy them on the internet."

He had an answer for everything when it came to the boys in blue.

"The robbers have kept things completely quiet since then, near as I can tell," I said. "Which also suggests they're pros. I've put out feelers all over town, but nobody has heard anything about who these guys might be."

"But somehow *they* heard about you."

"I know, right?"

We pondered it a minute. Roz shifted in her chair, but said nothing.

"Guess you've made a lot of noise," Jack said finally. "That must've attracted their attention."

"Just trying to cover all the bases, like I said, being thorough."

"Hoping to stumble across the robbers in the process."

"I guess you could put it that way."

"Sounds like you're no closer to finding them."

I couldn't argue.

Chapter 24

Felicia was waiting just inside the front door when I got home two hours later. Her face was flushed and her brown eyes were fierce and bright.

"Hi," I said. "What's wrong?'

"Like you don't know."

I played dumb. It comes easy to me.

"What are you talking about?"

"The Planning Commission meeting."

"Oh, that's right. That was this afternoon. How did it go?"

She frowned. "You really don't know?"

"How would I know? I've run all over town all day, interviewing people, getting nowhere. I haven't had time to think about the Planning Commission."

More frowning from Felicia. I kept my face as blank as a blanket.

"The meeting was a dud," she said finally. "Vargas didn't show up and neither did Donovan. They sent some junior lawyer who asked that the matter be postponed until next month. The Planning Commission was happy to grant the request."

"So it's on hold?"

"Officially. But I got the feeling the subdivision approval's a done deal. The only thing keeping them from steamrolling through the process was the fact that was I sitting there."

"Huh," I said.

"It's like somebody *warned* them that I'd be there."

"Not me," I said quickly. "I haven't talked to Vargas or Donovan."

Which was, technically, true. I'd let Gary Pierce do the warning. Felicia undoubtedly would figure that out eventually, but I was in no hurry. Let her settle down some first.

I offered up a distraction: "Want a beer?"

"Might as well," she said. "I'm not writing a story tonight. The Planning Commission postponed the one interesting item. The rest was rubber-stamp stuff."

I slipped past her and went to the kitchen. When I returned with two Heinekens, she was on the sofa, her feet up on the coffee table. Not relaxed, though. Still steaming. Maybe a cold beer would help.

We took a few soothing slugs before we resumed the conversation.

"Even if the commission approves Milagro Estates," I said, "that's only the first step, right? If your theory holds up, the subdivision is a bluff anyway. What they really want is to sell the land to the city at a big profit."

"That's right."

"But the bluff's no good until they've got the Planning Commission approval. You've got another month to stop it."

Some of the steam went out of her.

She smiled a little, like she was pleased and surprised that I'd paid attention when she talked about her investigation. Which, of course, was the effect I was going for. I get caught not listening often enough. I try to take advantage when I can. But now that I'd made the point, I thought I ought to shut up before I tripped over something.

Felicia seemed to read these thoughts on my face, which didn't help my cause any. She sighed.

"If I had any proof of the behind-the-scenes dealings, I'd take it right to the commission," she said. "But that's the problem with backroom stuff. No records, no proof they've even talked to each other about the development. All I've got is suppositions and poker games."

I nodded and took another drink.

"Too bad those robbers stole all the phones. Think what you could do with those."

Her eyes lit up for a second, then the glow died.

"They probably wouldn't do me any good," she said. "They'd have passwords and hidden stuff I wouldn't know how to navigate. We'd have to hire an expert to crack them. No way the publisher would spring for that."

I thought about my earlier conversation with Gary Pierce, when we talked about Goatface's phone.

"What about the police?" I said. "They've got the expertise, right?"

"I think so," she said. "But they'd need a subpoena if they wanted to use it to prosecute someone."

I took another sip before I said, "Goatface seemed very concerned about his missing phone."

"I'll bet he is," Felicia said. "The thieves could sell it to the highest bidder."

"That might be the police, too."

"No wonder Goatface is worried."

We both pondered that for a minute, then I got up to fetch us another round of beers. That sort of broke the spell, allowing us to change the subject.

Felicia followed me into the kitchen and we started heating up some takeout leftovers and we stopped talking about Goatface and the poker game and the Planning Commission disappointment.

But a couple of times during the evening, long after we'd moved on, I caught Felicia watching me, like she was waiting for me to crack and spill the truth.

Not for the first time, I prayed that I didn't talk in my sleep.

Chapter 25

A good night's sleep did us both a world of good, and Felicia seemed in a sunny mood as she left for the *Gazette* on Thursday morning. If she still suspected that I'd warned the Milagro Estates developers about her, she didn't let on. That made me uneasy.

I didn't have long to worry about it, though, because I needed to get halfway across town. I wanted to catch Cassandra Lyle before she left for her office. She wouldn't talk to me when Gary Pierce was around, I figured, but she might open up in a one-on-one situation.

I threw on a fresh version of the clothes I'd worn the day before – a pale blue shirt instead of a white one – and threw myself out into the rapidly warming day. It was supposed to hit the mid-90s again, and there was no sign of the thunderstorms that often keep Albuquerque from getting too hot in the summer. Not a cloud in the turquoise sky.

I still needed the baseball cap to keep my forehead bruise from being a topic of conversation everywhere I went. The visor shaded my face, and I wore dark sunglasses, but it still felt like the sun was too bright. I might've had a trace of a hangover from the beers the night before, but I blamed the sun for making me squint.

Cassandra Lyle lived in a Tramway Boulevard condo, an adobe brick of a building wedged among the granite boulders at the foot of the Sandia Mountains.

Great views, if you didn't mind the squint-inducing sunshine. From her parking lot, I could see across the great bowl of the Rio Grande valley, the urban sprawl overflowing its edges like sloshed soup.

I hadn't called ahead, so I wasn't surprised that it took her a while to answer the doorbell. When she did, she opened the door only a couple of inches, keeping it on its security chain. From what I could see of her, she appeared ready for the workday, wearing heels and a navy blue dress. Her dark, glossy hair looked freshly brushed.

"Yes?"

"Good morning. My name is Bubba Mabry. I'm a private investigator doing some work for Gary Pierce."

Recognition flashed in her dark eyes. "You were at the office."

"Right."

"I recognize the hat."

"Ah. Man needs a hat on a hot day like today."

She didn't take the hint and invite me indoors. She kept the door chain in place. I understood about security – a woman home alone, etc. – but I didn't want to conduct this interview through a two-inch crack. I tried to think of something that would set her at ease.

"Did I catch you at a bad time?"

I tried to see past her, but it was all shadows in there.

"I was just leaving for work," she said. "Why didn't you look for me at the office? Instead of driving all the way up here?"

"I thought talking in private might be better."

"Oh, really?"

"In case you didn't want Gary to know."

Her eyes widened, or at least the one I could see through the gap did. I assumed the other one went along.

"I don't have any secrets from Gary," she said.

"You want to call him and see if it's okay to talk to me? I understand."

The wide eye again. Like she kept being surprised by the things that came out of my mouth. Sometimes, I'm surprised, too.

"Gary's my boss," she said. "But he doesn't tell me how to run my life."

I glanced around the condo compound, but I didn't see anyone who might be listening. Still, I spoke at a whisper.

"You have a personal relationship outside of work," I said. "Gary told me that much already."

The gap narrowed an inch, like she was fighting off the urge to slam the door in my face.

"I'm not interested in that," I said quickly. "I only want to talk about Sunday's poker game."

She said nothing, studying me for a moment. Then she closed the door and I heard the rattle of the chain. She swung the door open and turned away, letting me follow her into the living room.

The sunny room was perfectly staged, everything in its place, clean and bright. Pale gray upholstery covered the low furniture. Yellow throw pillows served as splashes of color. Modern art graced the walls. The room looked like a picture scissored right out of a home-decorating magazine. I was afraid to sit on the furniture.

Cassandra had no such qualms, of course, and she settled onto a sofa, crossing her legs and knitting her fingers, waiting. I perched on the edge of a matching armchair.

"I'm not trying to drag you into anything," I said. "I'm only interested in the poker game and how it got robbed."

Her perfect eyebrows rose in perfect unison, but she didn't say anything.

"I know Gary told you about the holdup. It's my job to figure out how the robbers knew the poker game was happening at that vacant house."

I took a deep breath, but before I could continue, she said, "I was there that day. Is that what you're getting at?"

I had to blow out that breath and start over. "Gary told me that you helped him set up the refreshments before the game."

She nodded, but she didn't seem eager to say anything more.

"Did you notice anything while you were there?"

"Like what?"

"Like somebody watching the house. A car parked on the street nearby. Anything like that?"

"No. It's a very quiet neighborhood. That's one of its selling points."

"Right. And nobody followed you there?"

"Of course not. Who would be following me?"

Mrs. Gary Pierce came to mind, but I didn't say so.

"Did you know it was going to be a card game?"

"Not until I got there and saw that Gary had taken delivery of a poker table. He'd told me he was showing the house to some special clients."

"That was true, in a way. Lots of money sitting around that table."

"That's who we cater to. Especially Gary. It's a fickle clientele. We have to do everything we can to keep them happy."

"High risk, high reward," I said.

"Exactly. It explains why Gary has seemed so strung-out since Sunday night. The others probably blame him for the robbery."

"They have me for that," I said. "I was supposed to be providing security."

"Ah. So you're trying to redeem yourself."

Mostly, I was trying to keep Goatface off my neck, but I didn't tell her that. Let her believe that my motives were pure.

"After you helped Gary set up for the game, where did you go?"

"I came straight home. I wanted a shower and some quiet time. My weekend was nearly over. I expected it to be a busy week at the office, and it has been."

She made a point of looking at her wristwatch.

"You didn't talk to anybody on the phone while you were driving home? Texting to a girlfriend, your mom, anything like that? Or once you got home?"

"No. What are you talking about?"

"Somebody overheard something. Or somebody leaked something. That's how those robbers found out about the poker game."

"I didn't see anybody else after I saw Gary, and I didn't talk to anyone on the phone. I didn't even know about the robbery until he told me the next day."

I nodded. Before I could think of another question, Cassandra said, "I'm sorry, Mr. Mabry, but I really need to get to work now."

"Of course. Thank you for your time."

I got to my feet and so did she. She followed me to the door. I had my hand on the doorknob when I turned back to her.

"Is it common knowledge at the office? About you and Gary?"

"No. And I'd like to keep it that way. I don't know if there's any kind of future for Gary and me, but if there is, I don't want it tainted by scandal. Neither does he. He's got his kids to think about."

I swung the door open, letting the bright sunshine spill inside. It illuminated Cassandra like a flattering spotlight.

"I'm staying focused on the holdup," I said. "The rest is between you and Gary."

"Thank you," she said as I stepped outside.

She closed the door softly, then I heard the rattle of the security chain being put back in place.

Chapter 26

I called Gary's cell phone while I tooled along in the morning traffic. I hoped to catch him before Cassandra had a chance to tell him I'd been snooping around. He didn't answer, so I called his office.

I expected the old lady, Zelda, to stonewall me, but I got lucky, calling so early. The phone was answered by one of the other real estate agents, a friendly woman who told me that Gary was expected to arrive late this morning because he was first meeting a client.

"Oh, that's probably me," I lied. "I'm supposed to meet him, but I've lost the address."

"Hang on," she said. "Let me check the computer log."

I changed lanes while I waited, pushing into a crowded lane that immediately stopped moving.

"Here it is." She rattled off an address near the Albuquerque Country Club. I recognized it right away as the poker house.

"That's right," I said. "I couldn't remember the number."

I thanked her and got off the phone before she could see through my lies.

The change of destination meant that I needed back in the lane I'd just vacated, so I turned on my blinker and squeezed over. Somebody honked behind me.

I took I-40 west to the Rio Grande Boulevard exit, then went south as if going to Old Town. I bypassed the tourist attraction in favor of crossing over Central Avenue into the posh neighborhood beyond. Within minutes, I was pulling up to the vacant house.

Gary's ruby-red Corvette was parked at the curb, but I didn't see any vehicle nearby that might've belonged to a client. I parked behind Gary, then climbed out of the Olds and walked across the lawn and up onto the front porch of the flat-roofed house. A light breeze fluttered the leaves of the cottonwoods, but the temperature was rising with the blazing sun.

The curtains were drawn over the front windows, so I couldn't see inside. I rapped on the wooden door with my knuckles.

No answer. I tried the knob and it turned. I poked my head through the doorway and called Gary's name. Silence.

"Maybe he's in the back yard," I muttered.

It felt creepy to enter the empty house without permission, but there was no one to ask, so I went inside, tiptoeing around, looking for Gary.

I found him in the sunny dining room, near the back door, lying on the floor in a pool of blood.

"Shit!" I exclaimed.

I sprang backward a good three feet, and the rubber heel of my sneaker caught on the hardwood floor. I lost my balance and landed on my ass. Hard. It didn't knock the wind out of me, exactly, but I felt as if I'd been knocked senseless. Make of that what you may.

Gary lay on his right side, his arms before him as if he'd been reaching for the back door and never quite made it. His white shirt was mostly red, sopping with blood, and the tennis tan had drained from his limp, sallow face.

I sat staring at him for a minute, dumbfounded. Then it occurred to me to check that he was actually dead. I'm squeamish about blood and bodies, but I crawled over to the edge of the blood puddle and reached out to touch his neck. No pulse, and the skin was cool to the touch already.

Not much question about what killed Gary. He had two round red bullet holes in his shirt near his sternum. Now that I was closer, I could see blood in his hair, too. Whoever shot him had put one in his temple, as insurance. The fact that his head wasn't splattered all over the floor told me it had been a small-caliber gun. I imagined the bullet bouncing around inside Gary's skull, turning his brains into mush. It made me sick to my stomach.

Feeling that I might upchuck, I turned away from Gary and concentrated on my new phone. Most people, in such circumstances, would dial 911, but I had a friend on the APD homicide squad. I called the personal cell phone of Lieutenant Steve Romero.

"Bubba!" It always unnerves me when Romero does that. I know he's just seeing my name on the phone's Caller ID, but Romero usually seems all-knowing and all-seeing. Why should it be any different over the phone?

"Hi there," I said. "I'm, uh, calling in an official capacity."

"Uh-oh."

"I just found a body. A client of mine. Somebody shot him three times."

"Did you see who did it?"

"No, I just got here."

"Where is 'here?'"

I told him the address.

"Down by the country club?"

"Right. There's a 'For Sale' sign out front."

"It's vacant?"

"Yeah, the dead man was in real estate."

"Gotcha. Are you in the house right now?"

"Yes."

"Anyone else there?"

"No. Just the body."

"Go outside. I'll meet you in the front yard."

He clicked off. I put the phone in my pocket and wandered around the empty house for a minute. I don't know what I expected to see, but whatever it was, I didn't see it. I avoided going back into the room where Gary's body lay, and instead went out the front door, where a couple of ancient cottonwoods shaded the lawn.

I was leaning against one of those trees, my hands in plain sight, when the first patrol car rolled up.

Chapter 27

The uniformed officers didn't cuff me, but they locked me in the back seat of their cruiser while we waited for Lieutenant Steve Romero. The seat was hard plastic, and it seemed slightly damp, as if it had recently been hosed off.

Romero rolled up ten minutes later in an unmarked white Ford sedan. Everyone seemed to recognize him right away. He's a square-shouldered guy who wears short-sleeved *guayabera* shirts year-round. He's got hawk eyes that can see through bullshit and a mind that's an open-jawed trap. I've known him for twenty years – he was best man at our wedding – and I've always felt he was at least one step ahead of me.

He spent some time as head of the Homicide Division, but soon found he was more suited to murder scenes. He turned the management of the department back over to lesser mortals, and focused on what he does best. He's seemed happier since, but then he's always surprisingly cheerful, given his line of work.

Romero opened the back door of the squad car and let me out. I stood on the sidewalk and stretched, though I hadn't spent that long in the stuffy car.

"Hi, Bubba," he said. "Where's the stiff?"

"Inside. I'll show you."

"Just tell me. I'll go see for myself."

"He's in the dining room. Near the back door."

Romero nodded and strolled toward the house, muttering instructions to the cops who were standing around as he passed. They got busy stringing yellow "crime scene" tape around the yard. Other cops arrived, and a forensics lab van, and a couple of TV trucks. Pretty soon, the curbs were lined with vehicles.

I waited on the sidewalk, resisting the urge to jump into the Olds and drive away. The death of Gary Pierce meant a shit-storm was headed my way. Goatface Odell and the others would make my life hell. Not to mention Romero, who looked less cheery when he emerged from the house after fifteen minutes or so.

He paused on the front step, surveying the crowded street until his gaze settled on me. It made me gulp.

Romero ducked under the yellow tape and joined me on the sidewalk.

"Nice car," he said.

I knew he didn't mean the Olds. We both cast loving looks at the red Corvette.

"That belongs to Gary. Or it did."

"Gary Pierce? Our victim inside?"

"That's right. Nice guy. I've done work for him off and on for years."

"Any idea who plugged him?"

I shook my head, which was so busy with such ideas it's a wonder it didn't audibly buzz.

"I called his office and a woman there said he was meeting a client at this address," I said. "So I drove over, thinking I'd catch him here. I only needed a few minutes of his time."

"For what?"

"Progress report."

Romero smiled. "You had progress to report?"

"Not much. But I was hoping he'd write me a check."

"Ah. That sounds more like you."

I shrugged. When he's right, he's right.

"No one else around when you got here?"

"No. But I recognized Gary's car, so I knocked on the door. It was unlocked, so I went inside, calling his name. And there he was on the floor."

"You touch the body?"

"I put a couple of fingers on his neck, checking for a pulse, but that's all."

Romero looked me up and down, like he was checking for blood. Finding none, he said, "We've got your fingerprints on file."

"Yep."

"Who was the client?" he asked.

"Which client?"

"The one Pierce was meeting."

"I don't know. His office can probably tell you."

"What about his wife?"

That question threw me a little.

"What about her?"

"Did you call her and let her know he's dead?"

"I've never met Gary's wife. I don't want to be the one to give her the bad news. Isn't that *your* job?"

He scowled at that remark. It made me want to chew off my own lips.

"You know what I mean," I said. "Don't you want to be the one to break the news? To see how she reacts?"

He cocked an eyebrow. "You have some reason to suspect the wife?"

"No, no," I said quickly. "I told you, I've never met her and I don't know anything about her. I barely knew Gary."

"Strictly business, huh?"

"Nothing regular. Just once in a while."

Romero crossed his arms over his broad chest, the way he does sometimes right before he drops the hammer. I braced myself.

"And what are you investigating for him now?"

I flinched. The one question I didn't want to answer, which meant it was guaranteed to be asked, early and often. No sense lying any more than necessary. I've learned over the years that there are two people who almost always see through my prevarications: Felicia and Steve Romero. When dealing with them, it's usually best to just tell the truth and get it over with.

"Gary hired me last weekend to act as door security at a poker game."

"A private game?"

"Yeah, and that's a problem. Because the guys in that technically illegal game are well-known around town."

"So?"

"The game was right here at this house," I said. "Sunday night."

He looked back at the house. The front door stood open. Cops and crime-scene technicians went in and out.

"Why did they need door security?" he asked.

"Lot of cash on hand," I said. "The game had a thousand-dollar buy-in."

He whistled.

"How many people in the game?"

"Six."

"Including Gary Pierce?"

"He was the host. He was the listing agent for this house, and he was showing it off to the guys in the game. Gary had a poker table set up in the living room. All the drapes were closed. Nice, quiet neighborhood."

"So what happened?"

"Did you notice how the front door frame is brand-new?"

"Of course I noticed."

"That's because three armed men bashed their way through the locked door and held up everyone at the game."

Romero's eyes widened. I consider it a personal victory whenever I surprise him in any way.

"They wore masks and gloves. They had a Glock and a couple of riot guns. And they used a battering ram on the door."

"Jesus."

"Very loud," I said. "Caught me off-guard. I was sitting on a stool by the door, and I didn't stand a chance."

I took off my Isotopes baseball cap and let him get a load of my lump.

"Ouch."

"Shotgun butt," I said, replacing the cap. "So I was kinda dazed for the actual holdup. The robbers took a lockbox with the buy-in money as well as everyone's personal valuables. Jewelry, phones, wallets. They took my phone and my gun."

"How embarrassing."

"Yeah. Some of the players sort of blamed me for what happened."

"Since you were security and all."

"Right. And they, um, *insisted* that I figure out who robbed them and get their stuff back."

"And have you?"

"Have I what?"

"Figured out who the robbers are."

"Not even close. Everywhere I turn, there are dead ends."

"And now Gary Pierce is dead."

I took a deep breath and blew it out.

"I don't know what that has to do with the poker game," I said. "I mean, some of the players seemed upset with Gary because it happened here, under his watch, so to speak. But nobody wanted to kill him."

"Somebody did."

"Right. But Gary did business with a lot of people. Or maybe it was something from his personal life--"

Cassandra Lyle flitted through my mind, but I tried not to let it show on my face.

"--that got him killed."

"You got a theory?"

"No, no. I'm just saying it might not be connected to the poker game."

He didn't seem persuaded, but we got interrupted by a patrolman who shouted from the porch, calling Romero's name. Romero told me to stand by. He walked across the lawn to where the uniformed cop waited for him. They went inside the house.

Once again, I had to fight off the impulse to flee. I'd already told Romero more than I'd intended about the poker game robbery. Next, he would insist that I tell him the names of the card players, and I'd have to refuse. Nothing makes me more anxious than stonewalling Romero. He's made it clear over the years that – friendship or no – he'll happily throw me in jail for refusing to answer his questions.

Romero emerged from the house and walked back over to where I waited on the sidewalk.

"Gary Pierce's office doesn't know who he was supposed to meet today," he said. "He just told them he'd be at this address. A woman there said a man called a little while ago, asking for the address, but I assume that was you."

I nodded.

"You don't have any idea who he was supposed to meet here?"

"None," I said.

But I was thinking about Gary's rendezvous with Cassandra Lyle. Maybe he had used the house to meet other women as well--

"Bubba?"

I snapped back to the present, realizing that Romero had asked me another question.

"What?"

"What's the matter with you?"

"Sorry. I got distracted. I have a headache."

"How hard did that guy hit you with that shotgun butt?"

"Hard enough. I might have a concussion."

"Did you see a doctor?"

"No. I just put on a hat."

Romero shook his head, but he was grinning.

"A headache's not gonna get you off the hook with me," he said. "I need to know who was in that poker game. We need to talk to each of them, see if they have any idea who killed Gary Pierce."

I was already shaking my head before he could finish.

"I can't, Steve. They made me promise to keep the police out of it."

"A little late for that, isn't it?" He pointed a thumb over his shoulder, to where a flock of flatfoots paced around the yard, looking for clues. "I would say the police are involved."

I'd expected him to say something like that. I tried for a compromise.

"Let me talk to my clients," I said. "Now that Gary's been killed, they may feel differently about cooperating with the authorities."

Romero frowned.

"You know what I mean," I said. "The stakes have been raised. It's one thing to keep a robbery out of the newspaper. It's harder with murder."

He said nothing, waiting me out.

"Can I tell them that you won't reveal their names to the news media? That might make them more cooperative."

He shook his head. "I don't make those kind of promises."

"They could be confidential informants," I suggested. "You can protect those identities, right? Seal the documents or whatever--"

"Tell me the names, Bubba."

"I can't. Not without their permission."

He sighed. He glanced over at the house, where he undoubtedly was needed. Then he looked at his wristwatch.

"All right," he said. "I'm gonna be here a couple of hours. Come see me at headquarters after lunch. We'll take your official statement. By then, you should've talked to your people."

I nodded, and started digging my car keys out of my pocket. I wanted to get moving before he changed his mind.

"Hey, Bubba?"

"Yeah?"

"Don't screw this up. Bring me those names."

Chapter 28

I drove until the crime scene was out of sight, then started looking for a place to park. I had a phone call to make.

The parking lot of the Albuquerque Little Theatre was empty this time of day, and I stopped in a shady spot on the west side of the building. I rolled down the windows and killed the engine. A block away, traffic rumbled at the intersection where Lomas and Central merge near Old Town.

I found Goatface Odell's phone number in my recent contacts, and listened to it ring three times before he answered.

"What do *you* want?"

Bad manners, but I let it go.

"Can you talk?" I said. "It's important."

"Have you got good news for me?"

"Just the opposite. Gary Pierce is dead."

"*What?*"

"Somebody shot him full of holes," I said. "At the same house where the poker game got rob--"

"Not over the phone, stupid."

I took a deep breath and blew it out, trying for calm. Then I started over.

"I thought it would be best to call you first and see what you wanted to tell the others."

A pause, then he said, "When did this happen?"

"This morning. Gary told his office he was meeting a client at that house. I went there because I needed to talk to him, too. But I found him dead."

"Who was the client?"

"So far, nobody knows."

Silence while he absorbed the news. Then he said, "Jesus, what a mess."

"The homicide detective and I go way back," I said, "but he's not cutting me any slack. He's demanding that I tell him the names of the poker players."

Another pause. This one seemed to be filled with peril.

"The homicide detective knows about the poker game?"

"Um, yeah," I said. "I had to explain what I was doing there, right? I didn't want the cops to think *I* was the one who killed Gary."

"So you just told them about that holdup? After I'd specifically told you to keep the police out of it?"

"Hey, man," I said. "Murder changes everything. There's no keeping the police out now."

"There is if you're not an idiot."

"That make you feel better? To call me names?"

"That's the least I'd like to do to you. Be glad we're not face to face right now."

I wanted to be nowhere near his goaty face, ever again, but I didn't say so.

"Don't you think that--"

"Here's what I think," he snapped. "You got your ass into trouble, finding that body, so you're going to cough up the rest of us to save yourself."

"That's not at all what I--"

"You will *not* give our names to the police. I forbid it. None of the men around that table can afford the bad publicity."

"I understand that. I've understood it all along. And I haven't told anybody."

Felicia flashed through my mind, but I shoved the thought aside.

"It's different now," I said. "They'll throw me in jail if I don't give them your names. I'm supposed to be interviewed after lunch--"

"Do *not* give that interview. Get a lawyer and keep your mouth shut."

"I don't need a lawyer."

"You reveal those names to the police, you're gonna need a mortician."

Another loaded pause. It's always an awkward moment when the client threatens the detective's life.

"Look," I said, "I'll do the best I can. Maybe they'll figure out that the shooting has nothing to do with the poker game. If so, they won't be so interested in the rest of you."

"I'm warning you," Goatface said. "If you let this get on me, it'll be the last thing you ever do."

I'd had enough.

"Don't threaten me. Not over the phone."

I made sure the call was safely disconnected before adding, "Stupid."

Chapter 29

With Goatface's threats ringing in my ears, I put the phone away and cranked up the Oldsmobile. The old gray car started on the first try, as if it sensed I was in a hurry. I made it to Nob Hill in ten minutes.

All the women in the real estate office, even the ancient receptionist Zelda, were in tears. I went straight to Cassandra's desk. She dabbed at her eyes with a tissue, but seemed to be holding herself together pretty well, all things considered.

"We need to talk," I said. "Somewhere private."

The only private space was Gary's glass-walled office, and it felt a little creepy going in there. We shut the door, but neither of us sat down. We stood next to Gary's desk, turned so our backs were to the rest of the office.

"I'm sorry for your loss," I said. "I always liked Gary, and it was a shock to find him dead like that."

"You were the one who found him?"

I nodded. "What did the police tell you about it?"

"Zelda took the call," Cassandra said. "She was told that Gary was dead and the police wanted all of us to stay here at the office until they talk to us about what happened. But we don't have any idea--"

"Somebody shot him," I said bluntly. "Three times with a small-caliber pistol."

She gasped.

"Any idea who might've wanted him dead?"

She shook her head, her dark eyes wide and wet.

"Any chance that it had something to do with what was going on between you and Gary?"

"No. His wife would never--"

"Did she know about you two?"

Cassandra dabbed at her eyes with a wad of tissue.

"I don't think so. Gary was always so careful."

"He have any other girlfriends?"

A pause.

"Not as far as I know."

"What about you? Do you have an ex who's still carrying a torch? A stalker? Anything like that?"

"No romantic entanglements. I've always been happily single."

I took that to mean that she preferred married men, but I didn't say so. None of my business. Unless it was the reason for Gary's murder.

While I was pondering that, Cassandra said, "Frankly, I'm more interested in making money than in making a relationship."

I nodded. Sounded like she and Gary had been a perfect fit.

"Gary was meeting someone this morning at that country club property," she said. "Was that you?"

"No," I said. "I went there on my own because I needed to talk to him. The front door was unlocked and he was inside."

Her eyes flooded again, but I kept talking.

"See the problem? Because he was killed at that house, the cops want to know all about the poker game now. They want me to tell them who was sitting around that table, and I don't want to do that."

"What are you going to do?"

"I'm not sure yet," I said. "But I wanted to start by talking to you."

"Why me?"

"Because, near as I can tell, Gary was shot while I was interviewing you at your condo this morning."

I glanced over my shoulder at the main office. The other women looked away, but I knew they'd been watching us.

"I'm your alibi," I said to Cassandra. "I haven't told the cops about you and Gary yet, but they will find out. You can tell them you were with me when he was shot."

"That means I'm your alibi as well," she said.

"That's right. I'll try to keep you out of it, but if they demand to know where I was at that time, I'll have to tell them I was at your place."

"Couldn't you just make something up? Tell them you were at home or something?"

"These are homicide detectives," I said. "People lie to them all day every day. They would see right through me."

She nodded, like she could see right through me, too.

"I just wanted to make sure we had our stories straight before you talked to the cops," I said. "If they ask where you were this morning, tell them the truth. If you stick with the truth, it's easier to keep your story straight."

She nodded again.

"Okay," I said. "I need to get out of here now. The cops will be showing up any minute, and they wouldn't like finding me here ahead of them."

I glanced at the other women in the office. Zelda seemed to still be sniffling, but the other two were watching me and Cassandra.

"You can tell your co-workers what happened to Gary, if you want," I said. "They might be more likely to back you up if you need them."

"You really think I'll be a suspect?" she said.

"At this point, the cops suspect everybody. The only way to get off their radar screen is to have a solid alibi."

"Which I have," she said.

"Right. And so do I."

I waited until she nodded. I wanted to make absolutely sure we understood each other.

"Okay then," I said. "I've gotta go."

The other women in the office openly stared at us as we came out of Gary's private office. Cassandra, flushing, went straight to her desk and sat. I made a beeline for the front door, hoping to clear the area before the police detectives arrived.

Sunshine hit me square in the face as I went outside, and I fumbled for my sunglasses. I went around the corner, to where I'd hurriedly parked the Olds when I arrived.

A parking ticket fluttered under the windshield wiper.

Chapter 30

Since I was already paying extra for the parking space, I sat behind the wheel without starting the Oldsmobile. I rolled down the windows and let the breeze take away some of the heat that had built up in the car. I was parked in the shade, facing downhill toward Central, where tourists strolled the sidewalks and colorful buses whooshed along the street. A good place to be my temporary phone booth.

First, I called Felicia and left a message that I wouldn't be home for lunch. And that I might be working into the evening as well. I didn't mention Gary Pierce or Romero or the homicide. She'd find out soon enough, and probably try to make a headline out of it.

Next, I dialed Oscar Glass, an attorney I sometimes turn to when I'm in trouble. Oscar is an old radical from the '60s, a white-bearded dynamo who has devoted decades to defending criminals. Oscar's central philosophy (and he has, oh, so many) is that no human deserves to be locked in a cage. He often takes cases no one else will touch, and he sometimes hires me to help.

Oscar's the man you want on your side when the cops start threatening jail. He throws all five-foot-three of himself headlong into the legal battle, demanding your immediate release, acting outraged at the injustice of it all. It's a terrific performance, one I've relied upon more than once.

He answered his cell phone the usual way, barking, "Oscar Glass!"

It always sounds like I've interrupted him in the middle of something more important.

"Hi, Oscar. It's Bubba Mabry."

"I know that! It says so here on my phone."

"Ah. Right."

"Do you have that money you owe me?"

That tripped me up.

"What money?"

"Hang on," he said. "Let me look in the computer."

I could hear him tapping on a keyboard.

"Could we not do this now?" I said. "I've got an urgent matter--"

"Seven hundred dollars!"

"*What*?"

"That's what it says here," he said. "We've repeatedly billed you for seven hundred dollars. I assumed that's why you were calling."

"When did I rack up those fees?"

"Last time I represented you," he said. "When your gun accidentally went off? In a restaurant, I believe?"

"In the *restroom* of a restaurant, but, yeah, I know which time you mean. That cost seven hundred dollars?"

"My time is valuable, Bubba. The clock is always ticking."

"Sure, but I thought I'd work it off, like I have in the past. We've traded fees before without--"

"Seven hundred dollars, Bubba. Think how many hours of investigating you'd have to do. Better that you pay me and we'll call it good."

"I don't have that kind of money just lying around, Oscar."

"Then you're wasting my time."

"When did you become such a capitalist?"

"After my accountant pointed out how many unpaid debts my firm carries for months or years," Oscar said. "My clients are a bunch of deadbeats."

I resented that remark, but I let it go. Fact is, I had forgotten all about the debt. It had been months ago, and I'd tried to put the humiliating accidental discharge out of my mind. I didn't even own that gun any more; the robbers had taken it at the poker game.

"I got you off without so much as a fine," Oscar reminded me. "No community service, nothing."

"I had to pay for the repairs," I grumbled.

"That seems only fair. If you shot up my place of business, I'd expect you to patch the holes."

He had me there.

"As I recall," Oscar said, "you paid that repair debt directly to the restaurant."

"That's right."

"But you didn't pay your lawyer? The one who worked so hard to get you off the hook?"

"Okay, okay. Your point is made. I'm sorry I forgot to pay you."

"'Sorry' don't pay the rent, Bubba."

This conversation was going nothing like I'd expected. I felt like hanging up and starting over.

"Listen, Oscar, I'm on a big case right now. If it pays off, I'll make a lot more than seven hundred dollars."

"I don't like the sound of that 'if.'"

"You know how these things are. The investigation might be a wash-out, especially if I don't wrap it up pretty soon. And the cops are involved now, so things are getting complicated."

"Ah. So that's why you're calling."

"I wanted to see if you were available this afternoon. I'm being officially interviewed by APD homicide detectives and I thought it would be smart to have you standing by."

A long pause.

"Did you already talk to these police?"

"Yeah. I've got nothing to hide. I found a body, that's all."

"'That's all.' Like that just happens every day."

I sighed. "More often than I'd care to admit."

"Do you know who killed this person?"

"No."

"You didn't have anything to do with the homicide?"

"No! I just wanted to talk to the guy, but he was dead when I got there."

"Who is this victim?"

"Gary Pierce. He was in real estate. Office in Nob Hill."

"Never heard of him."

"You'd remember if you'd ever met him. He would've tried to sell you a house."

Oscar made a barking sound that I realized was a laugh. Had I ever heard Oscar laugh before? Mirth was not his style.

"I might not even need you," I said, "but there are certain names the cops want me to name."

"And you can't do that?"

"Not without getting in deeper. The names are attached to some big shots in town. They could make trouble for me."

"More trouble than the police?"

He had a point.

"We'll see," I said. "The police investigation could go in a different direction and they could decide I'm not worth the trouble."

"As your attorney, I advise you to not to talk to the police at all. If you must do the interview, then have me at your side."

"So I can rack up another seven-hundred dollar tab?"

"Cheaper than bail."

I thought it over, but not for long.

"I can't afford you, Oscar. I'll talk to APD on my own. If they don't like my answers, we'll see what happens. If they're about to throw me in the clink, I'll call you for help."

Oscar sighed.

"Do what you must, Bubba. You know I'll come running to your rescue if you call."

"Thanks."

"But when your investigation pays off," he said, "I get the first seven hundred bucks you make. And whatever other fees you've run up. Right off the top."

"Absolutely."

"Okay then." He sounded like he didn't believe me. "I've got to go. I've got clients on hold on the other line. *Paying* clients."

"Ouch."

I started to ring off, but I had another thought.

"Hey, Oscar, one more thing. You know anybody who can fix parking tickets?"

"Are you kidding me now? Is that supposed to be funny?"

"Never mind."

I hung up.

Chapter 31

My stomach growled as I drove east on Central Avenue. I was thinking about fast food, something cheaper than Nob Hill's chic bistros, when I spied just the thing: a taco truck parked on a corner near a construction project. An entire block along the north side of Central had been cleared to make way for a four-story apartment building. The wooden skeleton loomed over the street, and men crawled all over it, hammering and drilling and yelling to each other.

It was a little before noon, so I beat the construction crew to the shady spot under the one tree still standing on the whole block, a mulberry that looked wind-worn and dusty.

The taco truck was an old RV that had been made over into a rolling kitchen, complete with a smokestack out the roof. It was painted in reds and greens, with its name – El Taco Superior – scrolled down the sides in gang-style goth lettering. The cook was covered in tattoos and the kitchen looked permanently coated in grease and smoke, but my food was ready in minutes, and it smelled heavenly.

I ate my *carne asada* tacos while sitting on the hood of my car in the shade. I washed them down with a bottle of real-cane-sugar Coke from Mexico. Might as well live it up. My next meal could be jail food.

I tried not to think about the late Gary Pierce and the rest of it while I was eating. I didn't want to spoil my own appetite. But thoughts intruded as I chewed.

Who plugged Gary? And why? Did it have to do with the poker game? Or was it a result of his sexual adventures? Did his wife do him in, or some other girlfriend fed up with his cheating? A small-caliber pistol like the one that killed him is called a "purse gun" for a reason.

Or was it simply business? Last time I talked to Gary, he'd seemed afraid of being cut out of some big-money deal. Could he have been secretly involved in Milagro Estates? Was he threatening to blow the whistle on the others?

Would the poker players who *were* involved in Milagro call the whole thing off, now that they knew Felicia was onto them? What would happen when Felicia found out that I was the one who tipped them about the Planning Commission meeting? Would she ever forgive me?

Gary's death overshadowed everything, of course, but I still needed to find the trio who robbed that card game. The other players might be willing to drop it now, rather than risk further involvement with the police, but not Goatface Odell. He'd made it clear it was my job to get his phone back. I had no idea how to make that happen.

I thought about the Mustache Brothers. Cops or robbers? Both? All I really knew for sure was they wanted me to mind my own business. I hadn't seen the black Ford so far today, but I had a feeling those guys lurked somewhere nearby.

Men in hardhats started lining up at the taco truck. They were dusty and sweaty and sunburned and overworked. I caught a couple of them glowering at me, a man who was clearly underworked, lounging in their one patch of available shade.

I wadded up my wrappers and put them in a trash can near the taco truck. Time to get moving anyway. I needed to go downtown and find Romero at police headquarters. Endure his grilling for however long it takes. Without giving up those names.

As I got behind the wheel, I felt fortified by the tacos. And they had contained so many onions, Romero would think twice about getting up in my face.

The Olds balked when I turned the ignition. I pumped the gas and tried it again. The engine caught, choked on the extra fuel and farted out an enormously loud backfire. The construction workers jumped at the sudden noise. Then they all glared at me.

I threw the car into gear and zoomed out of there.

Chapter 32

"How do you drink this shitty coffee all day?" I asked Steve Romero.

We were in a windowless, fluorescent-lit interview room at the Albuquerque Police Department's downtown headquarters, sitting across from each other at a gray metal table that was bolted to the floor. The top of the sturdy table held our two paper coffee cups, a tape recorder and an attached steel loop for anchoring suspects' handcuffs. I wasn't in handcuffs. Not yet, anyway.

"What do you mean?" Romero picked up his cup and finished the acidic brew. "Nothing wrong with this coffee."

"You must have a cast-iron stomach."

"You're changing the subject," he said. "Where were you when you called Gary Pierce's office?"

"In my car. I was on my way to his office, but the lady on the phone said he was waiting for a client at that house near the Albuquerque Country Club."

"And you knew which house she meant?"

"Yeah. As you know, I'd been there before."

"Back up a second. You called from your car?"

"Right."

"Were you driving at the time?"

"Yeah. No. I mean, I pulled over to make the call."

"Where was that?"

"Where I pulled over?"

"Yeah."

"I don't remember, exactly."

"You don't live that far from Gary Pierce's office, so it must've been right there in the neighborhood."

"Um."

"Unless Gary Pierce wasn't your first stop of the day."

He didn't smile, exactly, but his black eyes twinkled. I gulped.

"Well, you didn't ask me that, exactly. You asked where I was when I made the call. I was in my car, like I said. But, yeah, I had already done an interview with somebody."

"First thing in the morning," he said. "That doesn't seem like you."

"I wanted to catch her before she went to work."

"Who are we talking about here?"

"Cut it out, Steve. I can tell by the way you're looking at me that you already know."

He chuckled.

"Cassandra Lyle says you were at her house, asking about the afternoon of the poker game."

"That's right."

"You didn't mention that before."

I shifted in my chair. "I thought I might keep her out of it. But it sounds like she told you everything."

"She said you're her alibi," Romero said. "Which is a good thing for her because she'd be a prime suspect in the homicide."

"She told you that she'd been seeing Gary on the side?"

Romero nodded.

"And that she and Gary set up the poker game refreshments together?"

Another nod.

"So that's all I wanted to talk to her about this morning," I said. "See if she'd noticed anything at the house before the players arrived that night. But she had nothing for me."

Romero looked me over.

"Pretty fortunate bit of timing," he said finally. "For you and for her. You just happened to be together when her married boyfriend gets shot."

"It's the truth," I said.

"I believe you. It just seems convenient, you know? A cynical man might think that *you* had something going with Cassandra Lyle, and the two of you had him bumped off."

"Good thing you're not a cynical man," I said. "Besides, you know Felicia. I would never, ever cheat on her."

"Too scared?"

"Yep. And not ashamed to admit it."

Romero smiled.

"This morning was the first time I ever talked to Cassandra Lyle," I said.

"Yes, but there was a second time, right?"

"Is there anything she *didn't* tell you already?"

"She said you came by again, after you left the crime scene. The two of you talked in private, right there in Pierce's office, in front of all those witnesses."

I caught myself squirming and forced myself to be still.

"I wanted to warn her," I said. "I knew her name might come up, and I wanted to let her know that she should just tell the truth about my morning visit. You and your guys would've turned it up eventually anyway."

Romero shrugged off the compliment.

"She have some reason not to tell the truth?" he asked. "Was that the problem?"

"Just, you know, Gary's married and they were having a fling, and it looks bad. I wanted her to know that it was all going to come out anyway, and that she'd only make it worse by lying about it."

"And you needed to do that in person? Behind closed doors?"

"I could've called her, I guess. But that seemed a little cold-blooded, when she's grieving and all."

"You've gotten awfully thoughtful in your old age."

"I'm trying to be a better person."

"Never too late, I guess," he said. "You've still got a long way to go."

"Thanks."

Romero rested his elbows on the table and leaned toward me. He looked suddenly serious.

"Pierce's office said they didn't know who he was meeting at that house this morning. For the official record: Do you know who the client was?"

"No."

"You're sure?"

"Absolutely. Do you think the client shot him? Like, a robbery or something?"

"Pierce's wallet was in his pocket. It wasn't a robbery."

"Then what?"

"You tell me. The only thing that seems out of place in Pierce's schedule is that poker game on Sunday night."

"Those guys play every Sunday night," I said. "At least that's what they told me. It was the first time for me."

"And the game got robbed."

"Yeah, but I don't see how--"

"Did the others blame Gary Pierce for the robbery? Since he chose the location and provided the so-called security?"

"There may have been some bickering after the holdup," I said. "I was busy recovering from a blow to the head."

I lifted my cap to remind him of the bruise on my forehead. He nodded impatiently.

"Yeah, yeah. You were incapacitated. But you're okay now, right?"

"Sure."

"Then tell me who was in that game."

"Aw, Steve. Let's not go there."

"We're already there."

"They're really private about this poker game. If I cough up their names, they'll ruin me."

He stared at me, waiting.

"Look, you don't want to know," I said. "Trust me. There are political pitfalls here, Steve. You don't want to stumble into them."

He said nothing. I squirmed some more.

"These guys are big shots," I said. "They wouldn't risk it all to bump off Gary Pierce."

"Big shots got more to hide," he said. "And they often don't place a lot of value on human life beyond their own."

That sounded about right, but I said, "*Now* you sound like a cynical man."

"Tell me the names, Bubba."

"I can't."

"Sure you can."

"They're big-money guys, okay? A judge. Maybe a member of the City Council."

His dark eyebrows rose.

"I said, 'maybe.'" I didn't want him thinking too much about which councilman I meant. "I'm trying to impress upon you the level of participant here. If we blow up their weekly game, it'll cost us."

"Let me worry about that. Tell me the names."

I clamped my lips together before anything else could spill out. Romero waited for a while, but when it became clear I intended to say nothing more, he said, "All right, fine. For now. But that means you're in the barrel."

"What?"

"You're the only person we know for sure was in that house this morning. That means you're 'it' until we get a better suspect."

"Aw, come on, Steve. You know I wouldn't shoot somebody like that."

He shrugged.

"I was at Cassandra's condo when the shooting occurred. You said so yourself. You can't hang anything on me."

"We need someone to investigate. Right now, all we've got is you, and you're being uncooperative."

"Hey, I've cooperated on everything except the names of the poker players."

"Which may be the very thing I need to solve a murder."

"We don't know that."

Romero stared at me, but I kept still.

"All right," he said finally. "For now. The only reason I'm not forcing the issue is that it sounds like these names come with a whole herd of lawyers attached. I don't need that grief."

I nodded.

"We'll give it a little more time," he said. "But if it starts to look like this murder is connected to the poker game or that robbery, you'll have to give them up."

"I understand," I said. "I feel certain there's no connection."

"You'd better be right. Because if it turns out you're shielding a killer, you're gonna be in big trouble, Bubba."

Chapter 33

By the time Romero turned me loose and I hiked back to where I'd parked the Oldsmobile, it was after five o'clock and swarms of office workers were fleeing downtown. Traffic was thick, lights were red, and we got stopped by a Rail Runner commuter train that zipped past while we were at a standstill at the crossing. It took me nearly fifteen minutes to go the three miles to my house.

Felicia's car was in the driveway, which made me sigh. I thought I was done being interrogated for the day, but the fun was only beginning.

I dragged myself up the steps and let myself in the front door. Felicia was sprawled in her usual spot on the sofa, her lap full of paperwork, her hands full of colored pens. Hard at work.

She gave me a smile when we said hello, but it vanished when I took off my Isotopes cap and hung it on its peg by the door.

"Your forehead looks like a hard-boiled egg," she said.

"An egg?"

"Your bruise is turning all yellow and green."

I went over to a mirror we've got hanging on one wall of the living room and studied my reflection. She was right about the bruise, but I thought my face overall looked wan and drawn and weary. Exactly the way I felt.

I sighed and turned away from the mirror. Felicia said, "Rough day?"

"The roughest. You?"

"Not too bad. I'm making progress on my big story."

"That's great, hon. You'll have to tell me all about it. Beer?"

"Yes, please. I'm nearly done for the day anyway."

I slumped off to the kitchen and came back with a couple of beers. Felicia moved a stack of papers so I could squeeze onto the sofa beside her. We clinked bottles and I took a long, soothing swig. It didn't help much, but it was a start.

"Why so tired?" Felicia asked. "What have you been up to?"

"I spent the afternoon in the warm embrace of Lieutenant Steve Romero. He about wrung me dry."

"Romero?"

"He said to tell you 'hi.'"

"That's nice. Why were you being grilled by Steve Romero? Was there a homicide?"

"You haven't heard?"

"I've been busy with this stuff all day. Who died?"

"My client. Gary Pierce."

"Oh, I'm sorry to hear that. And it's homicide?"

"Shot three times," I said. "At that same vacant house where I got the bruise on my head."

"Wow. Who shot him?"

"No idea."

"But Romero thinks you're involved?"

"I found the body."

"Wow again. No wonder you look so frazzled."

I took another consoling swig, then I told her about finding Gary's body and calling the cops and being quizzed by Romero. Naturally, she seized on the poker game connection, too.

"What did he say when you told him who's in that game?"

"I didn't tell him," I said. "I refused."

She arched an eyebrow at me. "Romero didn't worm it out of you?"

"He tried. I resisted. We're probably not done with it."

"I'm impressed, Bubba. Usually, you cave in when Romero is asking the questions."

"He's really good at it."

She was smiling now, gloating. She'd been able to figure out the identities of most of those poker players, which meant she'd outdone Romero. So far.

"And this time, he just gave up? That doesn't sound like Steve Romero."

"I hinted that the players were heavy hitters in the community," I said. "He started visualizing all the lawyers in his near future if he went after those people."

"Ah. That explains it."

"I was just glad he let me go. I'm apparently the prime suspect."

"Really?"

"Until they find a better one. It gives Romero a lot of leverage. If I don't play along, he could arrest me."

"He wouldn't do that."

"He might, just to prove his point. If he did, it would turn our lives upside down. At least for a while."

"We'll manage," she said. "We always do."

Somehow, that didn't reassure me.

"What about you?" I said. "You said you made progress on your story?"

She brightened and told me about finding records of an old Spanish land grant given to a family of settlers back in the late 1600s. Felicia had traced the ownership *forward* rather than backward, reaching the point where the riverfront land got gobbled up by shadowy corporations a few years ago. I had trouble following it all, but she'd cracked shell companies and uncovered secret contracts, layers upon layers. She felt she was on the verge of blowing open the whole land scam.

"Everybody's dodging me, of course," she said. "All I get are junior execs and baby-faced attorneys telling me they don't know what I'm talking about."

"Which is probably the truth."

"Maybe. Or they're just saying what they're being paid to say, like at the Planning Commission."

I nodded. I didn't want to talk about the Planning Commission meeting. Too many hazards there. Instead, it seemed like a good time to absent myself.

"Listen, hon," I said, "if you're that close to breaking it open, you should stick with it. I'll be quiet and let you focus."

"Oh, there's no need to--"

"I have some internet research of my own to do," I said. "I'll make a sandwich in a little while and eat it in my office."

"You sure?"

"Don't worry about me. Focus on your project there. Shout if you need anything."

"Might as well make two sandwiches," she said. "I'll want something by then."

"You got it."

I sprang to my feet and snagged another beer from the kitchen before I went to my home office. As I passed through the living room, Felicia was already back to marking up her documents. She didn't even look up as I went by.

Which suited me fine. The more she focused on those papers, the less she'd think about me and my blatant betrayal.

I was in no hurry to have that inevitable conversation. My ears were tired.

Chapter 34

My research was mostly an evasive tactic, but since I was hiding at my desk anyway, I booted up the computer and started plunking around Google and assorted social media, trying to get a better sense of the late Gary Pierce.

I hadn't known Gary that well, and I doubt we would've ever become friends. He was an ambitious, hard-living guy. I tend to approach life at a slower pace, which partly explained why Gary died rich and I'm usually broke.

Some people turn ambition into money. Others have plenty of ambition, but can't put together the discipline and connections and hard work it takes to get rich. Then there are people like me, who operate at an ambition deficit. As long as I've got food and a roof and a little pocket money, I'm happy.

Guys like Gary have big appetites and expensive tastes, but they really want only one thing: *more*. I learned to live with less back when I was a bachelor, running my detective agency out of a cheap East Central Avenue motel room. I wondered if Gary had ever been truly poor, as I had been when I was starting out, and if that explained his drive to succeed.

I had to scroll through hundreds of real estate ads to find the occasional image of Gary that wasn't his standard airbrushed mug shot. The candid stuff, from vacations and office parties and ribbon-cuttings, showed more insight into Gary's lively personality.

I kept zooming in on photos, looking past his gleaming smile to the chilly distance in his sky-blue eyes. I got the feeling he was always looking around the room for a better opportunity.

My eyelids were growing heavy by the time I hit upon a photo that snapped me out of my scrolling stupor. It was the usual promotional shot of a groundbreaking – five dressed-up people beaming at the camera while they pretended to dig with gold-plated shovels. Gary was on one end of the line of shovelers and Cassandra Lyle was on the other, both showing off their great smiles. A couple of bald men I didn't know – city business development types who'd funneled taxpayer money into the project – also wielded shovels. In the center stood Sammy Vargas, his chest thrown out and his TV-commercial smile stretching his thin mustache. Sammy wore cowboy boots with his business suit, along with a bolo tie made from a chunk of turquoise that must've weighed two pounds.

I read the caption a couple of times before I realized the groundbreaking had been for the apartment building going up on Central Avenue, the site where I'd eaten at the taco truck.

Felicia had told me Sammy Vargas was involved with such a project, but here were Gary and Cassandra, too, happily posing for the cameras. The caption said they had arranged the sale of the land, which formerly had been occupied by decrepit old Route 66 motels, torn down to make way for the new.

In the background crowd, discernible only when I enlarged the photo to its maximum, stood a man who wore a Panama hat to shade his face from the sun. Most people would have had trouble making out the blurry image, but I recognized those goggly eyeglasses and that long, narrow face.

Burt "Goatface" Odell.

Was Goatface involved in the apartment project, too? He supposedly owned property all over town. Was he a silent partner in Sammy Vargas' land development deals? Such backing could explain how Sammy had managed to jump from car dealer to real-estate magnate in just a few years.

And Sammy turns out to be pals with City Councilman Carlos Martinez. I wondered whether Sammy and the others had poured money into the councilman's election campaigns over the years. What did they get in return?

So many connections around that poker table. No wonder they kept the game a secret.

I wondered if I should show the photo to Felicia. She'd see the connections right away. There was the murder victim, along with his illicit girlfriend and the local big shots and Vargas and Goatface. Three of the poker players in one photo.

I squirmed in my chair, trying to decide whether showing her was a good idea. It would only make her chase harder after the poker players, which was probably dangerous. On the other hand, it might make up for the fact that I had tipped them about the Planning Commission meeting.

Felicia called me from the other room, making me jump.

"Yeah?"

"I'm ready to eat now!"

I chickened out. I cleared the photo from the screen and trudged off to the kitchen to make sandwiches.

Chapter 35

Exhausted from my long day, I went to bed early and slept late. By the time I finally stumbled into the kitchen in my bathrobe on Friday morning, Felicia had already left for the *Gazette* and the coffee in the pot had cooked into black sludge.

I was starting a fresh pot when my phone started playing its jazz-piano tune in the living room. I assumed it was Felicia, checking to make sure I was finally awake, so I hustled in there and grabbed up the phone and punched the button to answer it.

"Hullo?"

"Mabry? Is that you?" Not my sweetheart's voice at all. No, it was the now-familiar bleat of Goatface Odell.

"Yeah." I stumbled back toward the kitchen, phone against my ear.

"What's the matter with you?" he said. "Were you *asleep*?"

"No, no. Just having breakfast. Why?"

"More like brunch, this time of day."

"Yesterday was a long day. I had some catching up to do."

"While you were catching your forty winks," he said, "one of my properties got raided by the police."

"What?"

I felt fuzzy-brained. I needed coffee. I paced around the kitchen while he talked.

"A building I own downtown was being used as an off-track betting parlor. The cops raided it at two o'clock this morning, arrested everybody in the place, confiscated all the money and equipment."

"Wow."

"Everybody bonded out by daybreak, but the arrests put that operation out of business. And the building is sealed as a crime scene for who knows how long. That's gonna hit me right in the wallet."

"Did the cops connect the building to you?"

"That's the thing. There should be no way. The ownership is buried under a couple of corporate entities and my name's not on the deed or any of the paperwork. But as my lawyers were getting everybody out of jail, the cops who raided the place were in the hallway, joking around, high-fiving each other. One of them said to the lawyers, 'Give our regards to Goatface.'"

His use of the nickname made me jump with fright, as if it had come out of my mouth rather than his own.

"After I heard about that," he said, "I spent a long time thinking about that gambling operation. I was *insulated* from that property, you understand?"

"Yeah, I get it, but--

"Only way for the police to connect me to that betting parlor," he said, "is if they somehow got their hands on my phone. I had several conversations recently with the guy who ran that operation. He was afraid the cops were onto him. Turns out he was right."

"But how did the police get your phone?"

"That's what I want to know," he said. "If you'd been quicker, maybe this wouldn't have happened. Instead, all my operations are vulnerable now. Everything I've built could be ruined because some two-bit robbers got hold of my phone and gave it to the cops."

"I wonder if they used it to get out of jail."

"My lawyers say no," he said. "But they don't know everything that goes on at APD. Maybe you can't find these robbers because they're already behind bars."

"You think?"

"Or, more likely, just one got arrested and dealt the phone, and the cops are still looking for the others. Clearly, somebody's still on the loose."

"What do you mean?"

A pause.

"You really are slow, aren't you? How long have you been a private detective?"

"Too long. Who's on the loose?"

"I'm guessing at least one of those robbers is still out there," Goatface said. "Don't you think that's who killed Gary Pierce?"

"*What?*"

"They couldn't very well have done that if they were in jail."

"Wait, did you say--"

"Come on, Mabry. Who else could it be?"

"I'm sorry. I'm not--"

"You discovered the body and you haven't thought about who killed him?"

"Well, sure I did. I thought about little else yesterday, other than keeping your names away from the police."

"Ah," he said, "at least you got that much right."

I let that sit there.

After a moment, he said, "Don't you think that's the most likely scenario? Gary Pierce was mixed up with those thieves somehow. They met at that house to split up the loot or have it out or whatever, and Gary came up the loser."

I had, of course, considered something of that nature when I was stewing over Gary's murder the day before, but I'd pushed it from my mind so Romero couldn't get at it. Why would Gary get involved with the robbers? He was so intent on hanging with the big shots, why would he jeopardize it?

"Mabry? You still there?"

"I'm here."

"You got a better theory?"

"Not yet."

"Don't hurt yourself, putting out all that extra effort. You need another nap?"

"I'm fully awake now, thanks. That always happens when I talk about murder."

Another pause. The word "murder" seemed to echo over the phone.

"Let the police worry about Gary Pierce and who killed him," Goatface said. "You get your ass in gear and see what you can find out about my phone and who has it now."

"Will do."

What else could I say? The only way to get Goatface off the phone was to agree to his demands. And I wasn't going to get any coffee until I got Goatface off the phone.

"Don't screw this up, Mabry. This is your last chance."

I didn't like the sound of that, but I said, "Understood."

I thumbed off the phone and dropped it into the pocket of my bathrobe, half-expecting it to ring again right away. But it stayed quiet. For a change.

I leaned against the kitchen counter, my arms crossed over my chest, while I waited for the coffee to finish. I stared at the floor, lost in thought. By the time the coffeemaker finished gurgling and hissing, I had an idea about what to do next.

Chapter 36

I washed up and got dressed, operating on auto-pilot while my brain turned over the possibilities. As I coaxed the Oldsmobile into starting, it was nearly eleven o'clock, late enough that I could show up at someone's house without calling first.

I'd wondered all along why such proficient robbers would bother knocking over a private poker game, when the most they could reap was maybe ten grand and a few fancy wristwatches. Now I was more convinced than ever that the robbery wasn't about money. It was about Goatface's phone.

The police must've gnashed their teeth over the years, seeing Goatface Odell behind so many criminal enterprises, but never being able to touch him. He was too smart for them, shielding himself with dummy corporations and high-priced lawyers. But imagine if they could get hold of his phone, override the password protection or whatever, and check out who he's been calling. They might finally be able to take down Goatface.

The Olds seemed to be running okay, so I sped onto Interstate 40, headed toward the mountains. No fast way to get where I was going, but a stretch of freeway would be faster than sitting through red lights on surface streets. Traffic was light this time of day, and it freed me up to think.

Goatface knew the value of his own phone, and carefully protected it in his everyday life.

If the police tried to get a subpoena for the phone, they'd have to put together enough evidence to persuade a judge. Any inkling of such an investigation would be enough to alert Goatface, who'd toss the phone into the Rio Grande. And everybody would start all over again.

But what if the cops *stole* the phone? They could dress up like holdup men and hit the poker game, rob everyone there so Goatface might not immediately snap to the fact that what they really wanted was his phone. Then, using his call records, they could track down various properties where illegal businesses were being conducted. They could tell the courts the arrests were the result of surveillance or undercover work, and they'd never mention the purloined phone.

How long before they arrested Odell himself, tying him to those enterprises and filing charges and making headlines? No wonder Goatface was in a stew, taking it out on me.

I checked my mirrors as I got off the freeway at Eubank Boulevard, but there was no sign of a black Ford following me. More and more, I believed the Mustache Brothers were cops who were *also* robbers. They'd ordered me to stop my investigation because they were worried that I'd tip Goatface and ruin their crime-fighting scheme.

As I drove north past strip malls and fast-food joints, I thought about how none of those theories accounted for the central question I'd been trying to answer for days: How did the thieves know about the secret poker game?

Somebody must've tipped them to the time and place, and that was why I now drove through the winding streets of a Northeast Heights subdivision to the home of Roz and Jack Tate.

I parked at the curb and walked across the wide driveway to the front door. No other people were outside this time of day and no cars rolled down the street. It was the very definition of a quiet neighborhood.

I rang the doorbell and waited, anxious about what was to come, but it was too late to change my mind. The door swung open and Jack Tate filled the doorway.

"Yes?"

"Hi, there." I took off my sunglasses. "It's me, Bubba Mabry. The private investigator?"

"Oh, right. Bubba. I didn't recognize you without your baseball cap."

"I decided my forehead bruise needed airing out. Along with some other things."

A frown flitted across his face, but he propped up a welcoming smile, and said, "Where are my manners? Come on in."

He held the screen door open for me. As I went inside, he rested his big hand against the small of my back, as if ushering me into the room, but I knew he was checking to see if I had a handgun tucked into my waistband. Sadly, I didn't.

"Hey, Roz! Look who's here."

Roz Tate came from the kitchen, wiping her hands on a white dishtowel. Like Jack, she wore jeans and sneakers and a blue T-shirt. Casual, sporty. The happy couple at home.

"Mr. Mabry," she said. "What a surprise."

Her face showed not the least bit of surprise, of course.

"Sorry to barge in like this," I said. "But I was in the neighborhood--"

A total lie, and Jack seemed to sense that. His smile went chilly.

"--and I had something I wanted to run by you."

"What's that?"

"A theory. It might take a minute."

"Of course," Jack said, as if once again remembering his manners. "Sit, please. Would you like some coffee?"

I shook my head. No more caffeine for me. I was jittery enough already.

We automatically took the same seats as the last time I'd been here: Roz curled up in an armchair across from me, Jack sitting between me and the front door. Be hard to get past him if I decided I wanted to leave. That thought made me hesitate.

"So what is this theory you've got?" Jack prompted.

I didn't feel quite ready, but I took a deep breath and plunged in.

"Remember when I was here before and I said those robbers could've been police officers? Because of the riot guns and the battering ram and all that. And they were super-efficient, you know? Like they'd had training."

Jack nodded, but his face was serious. Roz, naturally, was impassive.

"Then there were these two guys with mustaches who followed me around and warned me off the investigation. They seemed like police, too."

A crease deepened between Jack's eyebrows until they almost met over his nose.

"Sounds like you have a problem with the police department," he said.

"Not at all. I'm a good citizen. I'm glad we have police to protect us. They've pulled my fat out of the fire many times over the years."

"But?"

"But police get frustrated just like anybody else. Sometimes, they give in to those frustrations and bad things happen."

"Huh." Jack sat back in his chair, like he was floored by such a suggestion. "Is that your theory?"

"We're getting there," I said. "I kept asking myself why these pros would knock over a poker game when they could've put the same effort into robbing something that would really pay off. Instead, they went away with a sack full of wallets and watches."

"I'm sure it added up to a pretty good score," Jack said.

"Maybe so, but I kept thinking, perhaps what they were really after were the phones."

"The phones," he said flatly.

"In particular, the phone that belonged to Burt Odell. The police could make all kinds of arrests, based on what's on that phone. They've already started, raiding a betting parlor during the night."

I looked from Jack to Roz and back again, but they had nothing to say and their expressions were stony. I pushed onward.

"All along, we've thought the robbers must've had inside information. How did they know the poker game would be at that vacant house on that night? Everybody in the game claims they didn't leak it to anyone."

"That doesn't mean anything," Jack said. "People never want to own up to those kinds of mistakes."

"True. But what if it wasn't a mistake? What if somebody tipped the *police* to the game on purpose and some undercover types decided to mask up and knock it over?"

"Why would they do that?" Jack said. "If they wanted to raid the game, they could just knock on the door and arrest them. Private poker games are illegal in New Mexico."

"Technically."

"That would be enough to get police in the door. No reason for them to batter it down."

I nodded.

"I thought of that. But remember, they didn't want to arrest these guys. They just wanted to get their hands on Goatface's phone."

Jack shrugged. I could tell from his face that he didn't think much of my theory so far. He certainly wasn't going to like what was to come next. I turned to Roz.

"How long have you two been working that game?"

"Three years," she said. "Give or take a month."

Then I asked Jack, "And how long ago did you retire from APD?"

"Four years ago. What are you getting at, Mabry?"

"I was thinking how frustrating it must be to the police, knowing Goatface is out there in the world, breaking laws, making money, and nobody ever touches him. And then I thought of you, Jack."

"Me?"

"You must've seen right away who Goatface was. The untouchable criminal. And here he was, sitting down to cards with these community bigwigs. That must've been galling for you to watch every week."

Jack said nothing, but his teeth were grinding together. I could see a muscle throbbing in his jaw.

"Maybe you'd planned for some time to hand Goatface over to your friends at APD," I said. "Or maybe you just recognized an opportunity when it arose. But your aunt's death was the opening you needed."

Jack's scowl deepened. His face looked like a crushed paper bag.

"Don't you talk about my aunt."

"Sorry." I held up my hands to show I meant no disrespect. "I'm sorry for your loss. Really. But the coincidence is too big to discount. I think when you saw you were going to be out of town, you called your buddies on the force and told them it would be the perfect time to get their hands on Goatface's phone."

He tried to smile, but it didn't take.

"So *I'm* the mastermind behind the robbery? Is that what you're saying?"

"It's just a theory," I said. "It could've been her idea."

I pointed at Roz. Her eyes widened briefly, but that was all the surprise she displayed.

"Really?" Jack laughed, but it sounded forced. "You think *Roz* is behind it all?"

I shrugged.

"I keep thinking about how she sat through the robbery, hardly moving a muscle. You're one cool customer, lady, no doubt about it. But this seemed too cool. Like you were sure they wouldn't hurt you."

Roz stared at me, giving up nothing.

"You knew the robbery was coming," I said. "You were the only one in that room who knew."

She didn't reply. She turned her head a couple of inches to look at her husband. Some unspoken communication crackled between them.

Uh-oh.

Jack turned back to me and plastered a smile on his broad face.

"You got a lot of theories," he said, "for a fella with a big knot on his head."

"Maybe I'm finally recovering from my concussion. Or maybe that shotgun butt knocked some sense into me."

Still smiling, Jack shook his head.

"I wouldn't count on that, sport. Frankly, you're not making much sense at all."

"No?"

"Nobody's going to believe this fractured story you've dreamed up. It's too far-fetched."

I said nothing. He might be right, but I didn't think so.

"Let me show you something that'll clear this up," he said. "It's right here."

Before I could react, Jack opened a drawer in the end table next to his chair. He pulled out a snub-nose revolver, a heavy blue-steel model, looked to be a Colt Python.

He pointed the gun at my chest and thumbed back the hammer. The "click" chilled me to the bone.

Chapter 37

Jack Tate was very casual in the way he held the handgun, like he didn't care if it went off while pointed in my direction. I felt very differently about that, but he didn't seem open to suggestion at the moment.

I glanced over at Roz, but she was cool as ever, as if nothing ever surprised her. I wondered how that must feel. My whole life feels like it's been one surprise after another.

"You couldn't leave it alone, could you?" Jack said. "We gave you every opportunity to walk away from this. But did you walk away?"

I said nothing. He wasn't really looking for an answer.

"You did not," he said. "You continued to fuck around in things you don't understand, and now it's come to this."

He waggled the pistol at me. I flinched. I couldn't help myself. It made him smile.

"Bet you'd like to walk away now, wouldn't you?"

I gulped and nodded.

"Too late!" he said, still grinning. "We can't have you running your mouth all over town."

"I could be quiet--"

"No, you couldn't. The minute Goatface starts asking questions, you'll fold like a towel. Then his phone won't be any good to anyone anymore. He'll shut down all his operations and start over."

"He may be doing that anyway," I said.

Jack shrugged, still casual, like pointing a gun at someone in his living room was just another Friday chore, to be followed by a relaxing round of golf with his fellow retirees.

"Maybe so," he said. "But shutting your mouth could buy us some time."

I sat very still, but my heart was fluttering.

Jack seemed to be weighing whether to go ahead and shoot me now. I hoped he'd choose to preserve his living room decor rather than mess it up with my blood all over.

Finally, he said, "I need to make a phone call."

He leaned over to Roz, gently handing her the cocked revolver, the barrel unwavering as it pointed at me.

"Keep an eye on this mook for me," he said. "If he so much as blinks, pull the trigger."

Roz looked from me to Jack and back again. Then she nodded. She rested her gun hand on her knee. She seemed comfortable handling the heavy revolver, which made me extremely uncomfortable.

Jack jumped up and went into the kitchen. I heard the *beep-boop-beep* of him dialing a phone, then he stepped back through the kitchen doorway, holding the cordless phone to his ear while keeping an eye on me.

"Hey, it's me," he said after a moment. "I've got a problem here at my house that I need you to solve."

Jack listened for a second, then said, "The private investigator. The one you've been watching."

My heart sank as I recognized that Jack must be talking to one of the Mustache Brothers. They were the only ones who'd been following me around, as far as I knew.

"Yeah," Jack said into the phone. "And he's got a big mouth."

I resented that remark, but it seemed a bad time to mention it.

"No," Jack said. "You come and get him. Take him out of here in cuffs. If any of the neighbors notice, I'll say he was an intruder."

He listened for a minute, his face twisting into a scowl.

"What do you think?" he snapped. "Take him out to the West Mesa and leave him there. I don't want any of this coming back on us."

Another pause, then Jack said sharply, "Do it now."

The phone beeped as he disconnected.

"They're on their way," he said to Roz.

He went back into the kitchen to hang up the phone, and Roz's head turned ever so slightly as she watched him go.

I saw this moment for what it was: My only chance. I lunged at Roz, grabbing at the pistol with both hands. She pulled the trigger, and the bullet would've blown a hole clean through me, but the Python didn't fire. The web of skin between my left thumb and index finger was caught under the hammer, which hurt like hell, but it kept the gun from going off.

I wrested the Python out of her grip and fumbled with it, cocking back the hammer and prying it loose from my punctured hand just as Jack bounded angrily back into the room.

"Freeze!" I shouted.

He froze. Except for his mouth.

"You son of a– "

I didn't let him finish. I took careful aim and shot him in the left foot. His white sneaker exploded, and it was as if the noise of the gun came out of his shoe. Blood gushed from a hole where the top of his foot used to be.

Jack gasped and fell to the floor, grabbing at the wounded foot with both hands. Roz let out a little yip at the sudden boom of the pistol, but she didn't move from her chair.

I backed away, keeping both of them covered with the Python. Gunsmoke hung in the air.

"I'm leaving now," I said to Roz. "He's in no condition to chase after me. Do I need to do the same to you?"

Roz shook her head. Her cheeks were flushed, but she didn't seem afraid.

I had no doubt there were other guns in the house, probably one tucked away in every room. I kept my eyes on Roz as I backed to the front door and reached behind me for the knob. She didn't try to move from her chair.

Jack still thrashed around on the floor, holding his bloody foot. He cursed and threatened me, but I didn't answer.

This was no time to talk. This was time to run.

Chapter 38

I held the warm Python under my loose shirt as I sprinted for the Oldsmobile. No sign of any neighbors coming out to investigate the gunshot, but I didn't want to risk some busybody trying to shoot it out with me because I was carrying a gun. I was in a hurry. I had to get out of here before the Mustache Brothers arrived.

I got behind the wheel and keyed the ignition. The Oldsmobile coughed.

"Oh, no," I said. "No, no, no."

I turned the key again. A sputter, then the engine died.

"Not now!"

I cranked it again. The starter grunted and groaned.

"Come *on*!"

Movement in my peripheral vision caused me to look up. Roz Tate had come outside and was trotting across her driveway toward me, her blond hair bouncing on the breeze. She had a shiny pistol in her hand.

I rarely resort to prayer, but this might've been one of those moments. I certainly was muttering something through my teeth as I turned the key. The starter whined.

When she was still thirty feet away, Roz stopped and squared up, holding the pistol in both hands. Like she'd had lots of practice.

"Yikes!"

I fell over on the seat, just as she put two holes in my windshield. Bits of glass sprayed over me, stinging my arms and face and neck.

I still had my hand on the key, so I cranked it again, hoping against hope. The engine turned right over, as if there had never been a problem.

Roz fired again. The bullet skipped off the roof of my car and whined away.

I threw the shifter into "reverse" and stomped the gas pedal. The Oldsmobile surged backward. The tires on the right side of the car bounced off the curb, and I raised up enough to see where I was going.

I hit the brakes and spun the wheel so the car was pointing the other direction. Bullets pinged off the trunk as I sped away.

I took the first right, and the shooting stopped. I took another right and went a couple of blocks, until I figured I was more or less parallel to the Tate home. Then I parked the Olds in the shade of a curbside sycamore.

My hands were shaking as I dialed Steve Romero's number. He answered on the first ring.

"Hey, Bubba. Ready to give me those names?"

That made me mentally stumble, but I pulled myself together and said, "I know who held up that poker game. It was dirty cops."

A pause. Romero said stiffly, "Sounds like you want Internal Affairs."

"There's no time to go through channels," I said. "The cops are gathering in one place right now. At a house in the Northeast Heights."

I told him the address. He said nothing.

"It's the house where Jack and Roz Tate live," I said. "He's a retired police--"

"I know who he is."

"He was the one behind it all."

"He had a solid alibi," Romero said. "He was at a funeral in Oklahoma."

"That's why they robbed the game when they did. It was the one time he knew he wouldn't be a suspect. He told some cops about the funeral and they held up the game while he was out of town."

Another pause. Romero usually processed things faster than this. I realized he was being very careful in what he said.

"And they're coming together at Tate's house now? Why is that?"

"To kill me," I said. "I just got away from the Tates, but they'd already called those guys to come and get me. Jack told them to take me out to the West Mesa and leave me there. We both know what that means."

"Wait a minute," he said. "The Tates let you get away?"

"Well, they didn't 'let' me. I snatched a gun away from Roz and shot Jack in the foot."

"Really?"

"Yes, really. Then I took off, but Roz had another gun and she shot several holes in my car."

"Where are you now?"

"Waiting nearby. I didn't want to run into those cops as I was driving out of the neighborhood, so I parked to call you."

"Can you see the house from there?"

"No, but it wouldn't be too hard to get a better view--"

"I'll send a couple of patrol cars," Romero said. "And I'll get there as quick as I can. You'd better hope we can sort this out."

"Why do you say that?"

"You just confessed to shooting a retired police officer in the foot," he said. "That's assault with a deadly weapon. These police you're blaming for the robbery? They'll say they were at the house to arrest you."

"I was defending myself– "

"Stay out of sight," Romero said. "I'll get there as quick as I can."

The call clicked off, and I put my phone in my pocket. Then I picked up the heavy pistol and climbed out of the Oldsmobile. I looked the car over. The windshield was spider-webbed from two bullet holes, and there was a silver blaze on the roof. I walked around to the back of the car, and saw three holes punched into the trunk.

"Oh, come on," I said.

I opened the trunk and, sure enough, one of the bullets had punctured the spare tire.

"Perfect."

I sighed and shut the trunk, telling myself I'd been lucky. Roz could've hit the gas tank.

I was the only person moving around the suburban street. I stuck the pistol in my hip pocket and walked toward the nearest house, trying to look like I belonged there.

All of the houses were set up like the Tate home, with a three-car garage facing the street and the living area tucked behind. A lot of the driveways had vehicles parked in them, but this one was empty. I hoped that meant no one was home.

My plan was to creep into the back yard and peek over the fence to see if I could see the Tates' house. I wanted to keep an eye on the place while I waited for Romero to arrive.

When I reached the back of the house, I saw an even better vantage point. The back yard had a leafy sycamore that matched the one in the front. Some dad had built a treehouse in its lower branches, about ten feet off the ground. It wasn't fancy, just two-by-fours and weathered plywood, but it looked like it would hold a full-grown person.

Foot-long boards had been nailed to the trunk to make a ladder, and I carefully climbed up. The treehouse was smaller than it looked from the ground, about the size of a card table, but I managed to fold myself into the space. The top of the treehouse was open, but the plywood walls were three feet tall on all sides and I felt concealed.

When I peeked over the wall, I could see between houses to the next street. I was looking right at the Tate house as the black Ford pulled up to the curb out front. The Mustache Brothers bounced out of the car and headed for the front door. They were dressed in plain clothes – jeans and polo shirts and black sneakers – but each had a gun on his hip.

Roz opened the door and let the pair inside. I wondered if she had called for an ambulance yet, or if she and Jack were waiting to talk to the Mustache Brothers first. I pictured Jack Tate sitting on the floor, his bloody foot wrapped in towels, as he barked commands at the younger men. That sounded about right.

He no doubt would send the Mustache Brothers looking for me. I needed to find a way to keep them here until Romero arrived.

I pulled the Python out of my pocket and rested it on the low wall of the treehouse as I took aim at the black Ford. A long shot from here, especially with this unfamiliar firearm, but I pointed the pistol at the left rear tire and pulled the trigger.

The Python boomed. I must've blinked because it was as if the tire went instantly flat on its own.

"That ought to do it," I said under my breath.

I ducked out of sight as the Mustache Brothers came outdoors, looking around for the source of the noise. Only then did I realize what a shitty hideout the treehouse made. If they figured out I was up here, they could blast a lot of holes in the plywood walls.

I kept low, even when I heard the men cursing about the flat tire. They knew I was nearby, but apparently they couldn't tell where the shot had come from, because they didn't start shooting at me.

After a minute or so of silence, I dared to raise up for a quick peek. The Mustache Brothers still stood by their car, looking at the mortally wounded tire, as two flashing patrol cars zoomed up the block toward them.

The black-and-whites stopped in the middle of the street, hemming in the black Ford, and uniformed cops spilled out, their hands on their sidearms as they instructed the Mustache Brothers to raise their hands.

There was a lot of yelling. The men from the black Ford identified themselves as police detectives. The patrolmen demanded that they show their badges. The Mustache Brothers got badges out of their hip pockets, but it still seemed tense, like they might go for their guns at any moment.

They were still sorting it out when Steve Romero rolled up in a white Ford with a couple of other plainclothes guys I assumed were fellow homicide detectives. Romero calmly took over the scene, and it wasn't long before the Mustache Brothers handed over their guns. They were outnumbered, and they probably figured they would come out okay in an Internal Affairs investigation. They even went along when Romero ordered them locked in separate patrol cars.

An ambulance screamed up the street and stopped behind the cop cars blocking the way. The ambulance driver conferred with Romero, then the paramedics got a gurney out of the back of the ambulance and rolled it across the driveway toward the Tates' front door. The other two homicide detectives accompanied them.

I saw Romero was looking around the neighborhood, and I ducked behind the treehouse wall. I wasn't sure I wanted to reveal myself. Not when I might get arrested for shooting Jack Tate.

My phone suddenly tinkled some jazz in my shirt pocket, nearly giving me a heart attack. I pushed the button to answer, mostly to stifle the music, then saw the call was coming from Romero.

"Hey, Bubba. You okay?"

"Yeah. I, um, I'm hiding nearby."

"You can come out now," he said. "It's safe."

"I don't know, Steve. It doesn't feel safe yet."

I peeked over the wall and saw he was examining the bullet hole in the tire of the black Ford. He turned, measuring the trajectory with his eyes, and looked right at me.

I ducked down, but it was too late.

"Come down from there, Bubba," he said over the phone.

I put the phone and the pistol in my pockets, then slowly clambered down the ladder. By the time I reached the ground, Romero was standing right there, waiting.

"Give me the gun, Bubba. It's evidence."

I hated to hand over the Python, but he was right, of course. He used an ink pen to carry the pistol by its trigger guard.

I followed him between houses to the Tates' street. When the Mustache Brothers saw me, they bounced around in the back of the squad cars, barking and threatening, their faces red, their mustaches bristling. I was glad they were locked in the cars.

Romero handed the Python over to a gloved policewoman, who dropped it into a clear plastic bag and sealed it up.

Then Romero turned to me and said, "Now, Bubba, tell me what the hell happened here."

Chapter 39

I got right to the point.

"Burt Odell."

"Goatface?" Romero said. "What about him?"

"He plays in the Sunday night poker game."

"I thought you said the players were pillars of the community."

"The rest of them are, but they've known Goatface for years. So there he is every week, playing cards with the big shots."

One of the uniformed patrolmen hurried up to us, but Romero held up a hand like he was stopping traffic.

"Not now."

The patrolman scurried away.

"Jack Tate started working the door at these games three years ago. He knew who Goatface was, of course, and how badly the police would like to nail him."

Romero nodded.

"So, when Tate got called out of town for a funeral, he saw his opportunity. He called some friends on the force and told them it would be a good time to hit the game. They put on masks and battered in the door and robbed everyone in the place, but what they were really after was Goatface's phone."

"His phone."

"Apparently, Goatface uses it to make business calls."

"Ah."

"So it's a gold mine for these guys."

I pointed at the patrol cars, where the Mustache Brothers glared at me.

"That's Brody and Ferguson," Romero said. "They work Vice."

"Do they work undercover? Because those mustaches are a dead giveaway--"

"Get to the point, Bubba."

"I think these guys are two of the three who robbed the game," I said. "The third one's probably Vice, too."

"And they took this risk just to get Goatface's phone?"

"I'm sure they kept the cash and jewelry as a bonus," I said. "But the phone was the goal. They've already used information from it to raid one of Odell's properties. A betting parlor downtown?"

Romero nodded to show he'd heard about last night's raid.

"They couldn't come up with any legal way to get hold of that phone," I said. "So they turned to an illegal way."

"Can you prove this?" he asked.

I thought about it for a second, then shook my head.

"I can't," I said, "but you can. Search that Ford. Search their desks. Search their homes. When you turn up Goatface's phone, the rest will click into place."

We were interrupted by the paramedics, who rolled Jack Tate past us on the gurney, headed toward the ambulance.

"Hey, Romero," Jack croaked as they went by. "Why isn't that guy in cuffs? He shot me in the foot."

Romero didn't answer. He turned back to me and said, "So you came here today and confronted Big Jack Tate? Accused him of being part of a conspiracy? All by yourself?"

"When you put it like that, it doesn't sound so smart."

Romero sighed.

I told him the rest of it – how Jack had gotten the drop on me, then taken a moment to call Brody and Ferguson, how I grabbed the gun from Roz and turned the tables on them. I showed him the bloody puncture in my hand where she'd dropped the hammer.

"Ouch," he said.

"Better than a bullet in the guts. I took the gun away from her and turned it around just as Jack came after me."

"And you shot him in the foot."

"It seemed the safest thing," I said. "I wasn't trying to kill him. I just wanted to get out of there before he could get his hands on me."

Past Romero, I could see the two homicide detectives marching Roz toward the cars. Her hands were cuffed behind her back, and she stared daggers at me until they shoved her into the back seat of their unmarked Ford.

"She followed me out of the house," I told Romero. "I was trying to get my car started, and she started shooting at me with a different gun."

Romero closed his eyes and shook his head, like he could barely stand to hear it all.

"I managed to get it in gear and flee," I said, "but she put a few bullet holes in the car."

"Where's your car now?"

"Over on the next street. I didn't want to go too far. I knew these guys were on their way to get me, so it might be the only time you could catch them all in the same place. I wanted to keep an eye on them until you could get here."

"So you hid in the treehouse."

"Right. And I shot out their tire so they couldn't drive away."

Romero looked to the treehouse and back to the Ford, measuring the space.

"That's pretty good shooting," he said. "For you."

Not exactly a compliment. I let it go.

"It worked," I said. "You got here in time."

"Lucky for you."

I nodded. If the police response had been slower, I'd probably be dead now. Brody and Ferguson would've found me in that treehouse and put a bunch of holes in me. Then they would've made up some story about me being a burglar or a peeping tom, and they would've gotten away clean. Because the police always get the benefit of the doubt.

"Which one of these guys was driving the Ford?" Romero asked.

"The taller one."

"Ferguson. Hold on a sec."

He went over to the squad car and opened the back door. Ferguson, grinning, started to get out, but Romero shoved his shoulder to show him to stay put. Instead, he demanded the keys to the Ford. Frowning now, Ferguson fished them out of his pocket and handed them over. He opened his mouth to add something, but Romero slammed the door shut.

We went over to the Ford. I stayed on the sidewalk while Romero checked out the interior of the car and the glove compartment. He didn't turn up a phone or much of anything else. He gave me a dark look as he slammed the doors.

I shrugged. I hadn't promised him Goatface's phone. I said it *might* be in the car.

Romero went around to the trunk and used the keys to open it. I followed him there and looked inside.

Two shotguns were in the trunk, along with a steel battering ram with welded handles.

"Look familiar?" Romero asked.

I nodded. "Believe me now?"

He sighed and slammed the trunk.

Chapter 40

The preliminary investigation took all afternoon. Romero handed off the lead to a couple of Internal Affairs suits named – I shit you not – Flint and Steele. I tried to make a joke about their names sparking my memory, but they'd heard it all before, and they clearly weren't joking types.

They walked me through the whole thing again, from the night of the poker game until this very minute. I told the truth about everything. I even gave up the names of the poker players. They recognized the names, of course. Flint went, "Whew," which is the most emotion either guy showed all afternoon.

After we'd covered it all twice and they'd taken pictures of everything in the neighborhood and my bullet-riddled car and the inside of the Tate house, we drove downtown, where I got to answer the questions again for the video cameras. I understood why the IA guys were being so careful. It's tough to sew up a case against other cops and their lawyers and their union reps. But I hated the video part. I could see myself on a monitor, my hair askew and my forehead bruised, and I looked like a madman, throwing out accusations. Guess it was good enough for Flint and Steele, though, because they let me go home just after five o'clock. They made it clear that they weren't done with me.

The sun beat down on me as I hiked to where I'd left the Oldsmobile.

Naturally, there was a parking ticket under the windshield wiper. I plucked it off and pocketed it without a word. I got behind the wheel of the car, which started right up, like it knew we were headed home.

All six lanes of Lomas Boulevard were jammed, but I tried to be patient. I told myself I was decompressing after all the excitement, and the traffic could not bother me. I took deep breaths and ignored the stares of the other motorists as they noticed the bullet holes in the Olds.

Finally, just past University Hospital, the traffic thinned. Too late to help me much, as I was getting off Lomas anyway, steering onto the quiet streets of our neighborhood. Before I even reached our block, I could see Felicia's car parked in the driveway. I took more deep breaths, trying to meditate away my anxiety. It's a wonder I didn't hyperventilate and pass out at the wheel.

I parked the Olds on the street, broken windshield and all, and shambled into the house. Felicia was in her usual place on the sofa, but there were no piles of documents anywhere in sight, and she was relaxed and smiling. She looked sort of *happy*, so I didn't know what to think.

"What happened to you?" she said by way of greeting. "You look like hell."

"Thanks. I spent the whole day with the police, explaining why I shot a retired cop in the foot."

That wiped the smile right off her face.

"You *shot* somebody?"

"It happens sometimes," I said. "Occupational hazard."

"It's been a while, though."

"Yeah. Anyway, I've been through the wringer today. I need rest and food."

"Did you get any lunch?"

"I ate a cheese sandwich out of a vending machine."

"That's not food."

"You got that right."

Felicia whipped out her cell phone. "I'll call for pizza."

"That's just more cheese and bread."

"I'll get pepperoni."

I was too tired to argue. I slumped onto the sofa next to her and wrestled off my sneakers while she talked to the pizza joint we always call. It's only nine blocks away, on Central, but we regularly have pizza delivered because neither of us likes to cook and we're too lazy to go pick it up.

After she got off the phone, Felicia leaped up and went to the kitchen to get us a couple of beers. I got the idea she might've been escaping the odor of my sweaty sneakers, so I tossed them across the room.

"I've had a big day myself," Felicia said as she returned with the Heinekens, "but I didn't shoot anybody, so I guess you get to go first."

The last thing I wanted was to tell it all again, but I took a slug of beer and soldiered through. I'd told the story so many times, I had it pretty well polished. I got through it in about fifteen minutes, ending with how Flint and Steele found Goatface's phone in Brody's desk drawer to seal the deal.

"That is a big day," she said when I was done. "You solved the case, Bubba."

"What?"

"The poker game robbery. You set out to solve it and you did. That's a real breakthrough for you."

"I solve things all the time."

"Of course you do, dear. I just meant this was a big one. Dirty cops. It'll make front-page headlines."

"The Internal Affairs guys told me not to tell anyone--"

"Relax, Bubba. I'm not going to race out the door and try to put together a story about your big case. It's too late in the day. I'd never make deadline."

She checked her wristwatch, like she was making sure.

"Besides," she said, "I've already got tomorrow's front page."

I know an escape route when I see one. I said, "Is that why you seem so happy?"

She nodded, smiling.

"Milagro Estates. I broke it wide open. And your buddy Goatface is involved in that, too."

"*What*?"

"I went back through everything, looking for traces of Gary Pierce after you found him dead."

"And?"

"Nothing," she said. "Near as I can tell, he was never involved in Milagro Estates. But his firm was. I found Cassandra Lyle's fingerprints all over the place."

"Oh, my."

"She shepherded through the paperwork to rezone that tract down by the river. Once I started looking for her name, it turned up in other places, too. Dummy corporations, leases to properties that don't exist."

"Holy cow."

"Cassandra's in it deep," she said. "Lots of these corporate entities trace back to the same person. Guess who."

"Goatface Odell."

"That's right."

"You're outing him in tomorrow's *Gazette*?"

She nodded.

"All his crooked businesses and contracts and stuff?"

"Not all of it, I'm sure. But we've got enough to make a big story. That'll bring people out of the woodwork, eager to talk to the newspaper about how they've been screwed over by Goatface. You know how it is: Once people start talking, everybody wants to get on board."

I took another slug of beer and said, "That may be the way it usually works, but don't be surprised if people refuse to speak against Goatface. Most people are scared of him."

"I'm not," she said.

"I know. You're not scared of anything. Does the poker game robbery factor into your story?"

"Not so far," she said. "I'm still trying to reach the people who were at the game."

"I wish you wouldn't."

"But they're the same people, Bubba! They have been all along. The ones I've been after are the same ones whose names you've been trying to protect."

"Yeah, but--"

"Sammy Vargas is right in the middle of the Milagro Estates scam, and so is his buddy Carlos Martinez. Tom Donovan's bank is backing the bogus development deal. Gary Pierce's girlfriend was involved, even if he wasn't. And Goatface is right in the middle of it."

I finished off my beer and set it on the coffee table. I sat staring into space until Felicia said, "What is it?"

"I was just thinking about those Vice cops. They broke all kinds of laws trying to get hold of Goatface's phone, trying to bring him down. If they'd just waited, you would've done the job for them."

We toasted her success, but I didn't feel celebratory. I might've solved the case of the poker game robbery and gotten some dirty cops thrown in jail, but I didn't have any idea who killed Gary Pierce. A capable detective, like the ones in the paperbacks I read all the time, would've solved Gary's murder while he was at it.

I opened my mouth to say as much to Felicia, but the doorbell rang first.

She said, "That must be the pizza. I'll get it."

She grabbed her purse off the end table and hustled to the front door. I stayed on the sofa, but I was thinking that it didn't seem like enough time had passed since she called for the pizza. Could the delivery be this soon?

Before I could say anything, Felicia flung open the front door. She dropped her purse when she saw who was standing there: Burt "Goatface" Odell. He was dressed in a double-breasted suit, wingtip shoes and a gray fedora, like somebody out of an old black-and-white movie.

The shiny little pistol in his hand looked brand-new.

Chapter 41

"Put your hands up," Goatface snarled.

Felicia did as she was told. For once.

"Now back up. Out of the way."

She moved back a few steps. Goatface came inside and shut the door behind him. He kept the little pistol pointed at my sweetheart.

I didn't move. Wrestling up off the squishy sofa was out of the question. Goatface could shoot me full of holes before I made it to my feet. And what could I do anyway? I had no gun, no weapon of any kind, not even anything I could hurl at him. The spindly coffee table held a couple of beer bottles and a fat hardcover novel Felicia had been reading for weeks, but it was all too far away to help me. The only item within arm's reach was a throw pillow.

Goatface gestured with the pistol, motioning Felicia backward, and she took a couple more steps back, stopping between the coffee table and the TV. He seemed to relax a little; now he could keep us both covered at once.

"You idiots," he began. "You fucking imbeciles. You've ruined my life with your fumbling around."

"Take it easy--"

"Shut it, Mabry. I didn't come here to hear you talk. I'm on my way out of town. I'm wearing my traveling clothes."

He tapped the brim of his fedora, like he was bidding us farewell. I didn't like the way that felt. Too final.

"I've lived in Albuquerque my whole life," he said, "but now you've ruined the town for me. The cops are raiding my properties. And I understand I'm going to be on the front page of the *Gazette* tomorrow."

Felicia's eyes widened, but she didn't try to argue.

"I'm not gonna stick around and wait for the cops to come for me," he said. "I've got a plane to catch."

My sweetie chose this moment to speak up. "Then what are you doing here?"

I cringed, but Goatface smiled.

"Unfinished business," he said. "I'm not leaving you two to talk about me when I'm gone."

A car door slammed outside. Goatface didn't seem to notice, but the noise gave me hope. I braced myself for action.

Felicia looked Goatface right in the eye and said, "Is that the same gun you used to kill Gary Pierce?"

My mouth fell open. *Goatface* killed Gary? Was that possible? Was it logical? Or had my sweetie taken one mental leap too far? Then I realized she was bluffing. A bold move, considering she was gambling with our lives.

"I was trying to talk sense to him," Goatface said, making me gape again. "He thought we were cutting him out of the Milagro Estates deal. He threatened to go public."

"So you shot him," she said flatly.

Goatface scowled at the interruption. He pointed the little pistol at her and said, "Just like this."

His finger tightened on the trigger.

Then the doorbell rang.

Startled, Goatface turned toward the door, the little gun straying from its aim on Felicia.

The moment I had been waiting for.

I kicked upward with both feet, hard as I could given that I wasn't wearing any shoes. The coffee table flipped over, launching the bottles and book toward Goatface. He threw up his arms to ward off the missiles.

It felt like I'd stubbed all my toes at once, but I ignored the pain and rolled off the sofa, landing on the hardwood floor on all fours. Which really hurt my knees.

I crawled toward Goatface like a crazed toddler. I expected a bullet any second, so I lunged forward the last few feet, hitting him in the shins with my shoulder and right arm. A nice tackle, if I do say so myself, and Odell fell, landing on his back on the hardwood floor. The air oofed out of him. His hat and his glasses went flying, but he didn't let go of that compact pistol.

I tried to lunge forward again, but I couldn't get any traction with my scurrying sock feet. I sort of flopped across Goatface's legs, reaching for his little gun with both hands.

The pistol cracked, punching a hole in the ceiling. Plaster dust snowed down on us as we wrestled on the floor.

I got hold of his hand and tried to twist the pistol free of his grip, but he was stronger than he looked. I shifted my weight, so I was lying on top of his stomach, squishing the air out of him while we struggled over the gun.

I wondered where Felicia was. I could've used some assistance with Goatface, but I hoped she'd run to safety instead. I hoped she was dialing 911.

Using all my strength, I twisted Goatface's hand, bending his wrist, loosening his grip. He responded by pulling the trigger.

The little gun cracked, deafening so close to my ear, and the bullet buried itself in my right buttock.

That's right, he shot me in the ass. Go ahead and laugh. Everyone does. But let me tell you, it hurts like hell to get shot anywhere, even in your most padded locations. The bullet felt like it was on fire in there.

Somehow, I hung onto his gun hand despite the shock of getting shot. Goatface tried to roll free and almost succeeded, but at that moment Felicia danced into the fracas, the wooden coffee table cocked back over her head. She crashed it down on Goatface's forehead, the corner of the table striking him right between the eyes.

Goatface went limp all over. I wrested the little pistol out of his hand and rolled off him, getting blood all over the floor from the hole in my pants. I dragged myself up, so I was leaning against the sofa, my weight on my unpunctured buttock, the pistol pointed at Goatface.

"You've been shot!" Felicia exclaimed.

I resisted the urge to comment on her mastery of the obvious. Instead, I said, "Call an ambulance. I'll watch this guy."

"Right," she said.

She hesitated, though.

"One sec."

Felicia snatched her purse up off the floor and went to the front door while I lay there, bleeding. She threw open the door. The pizza delivery kid still stood out there on the porch, holding his flat box. He was a freckle-faced teen in a red polo shirt and a paper hat.

"Were those gunshots?" he asked.

"Hammer," she said. "We're hanging pictures."

"What?"

She handed him some money from her purse, took the pizza, and said, "Keep the change." Then she shut the door on him.

"You paid for the pizza *before* you called 911?"

"I didn't want to leave him waiting," she said. "That kid saved our lives, ringing the doorbell when he did."

She was right, of course, but I was still a little miffed.

Goatface stirred at that moment, regaining consciousness. His gotch-eyed gaze landed on the pistol in my hand. He groaned.

I wanted to say something triumphant, but I was in shock from being wounded, and what came out of my mouth was: "Hah! I guess the glove's on the other foot now."

Goatface looked confused, and I couldn't blame him.

Felicia, phone to her ear, tapped me on the shoulder.

"Better let me hold that pistol, hon," she said. "Until the police get here."

That seemed like a good idea. I handed it over.

Goatface groaned some more, barely coherent, but finally managed to put together some words.

"Why," he moaned, "do I smell *pizza*?"

Chapter 42

The responding officers had a great time making fun of how I'd gotten shot in the ass and how I might have brain damage and how I'd have to get the lead out and how I'd be a double asshole now. Even the paramedics who got the bleeding stopped seemed to be smirking the whole time. Certainly, all my neighbors were entertained when the paramedics rolled me out to a waiting ambulance on a gurney. Given the nature of my wound, I rode face-down with my bandaged ass sticking up in the air.

Most humiliating of all was the morning *Gazette*, which Felicia brought to my hospital room the next day. Half the front page was given over to the lead story, which reported that racketeer Burt Odell was behind bars, accused of killing Gary Pierce and attempting to murder Felicia and me, and how his actions were tied to the Milagro Estates scam and a poker game robbery by three jailed Vice cops.

Felicia and I came off looking sort of heroic in the article, but nearly every reference to me mentioned the fact that I'd been shot in the butt. It was going to take a long time to live this one down.

Felicia hadn't written the article, of course, since she was one of the participants and had a whopping conflict of interest. The byline attributed the story to a reporter named Monica Lopez.

"I wish this Monica hadn't seen fit to discuss my rear end so often," I said when I finished reading the article.

"That was me," Felicia said brightly. "I told her to be sure to mention your gunshot wound at every opportunity."

"*What?* Why embarrass me like that?"

Felicia sat on the edge of my hospital bed, smiling.

"Payback," she said.

"For what?"

"For meddling in my reporting."

"When did I ever--"

"You warned Vargas and the others that I was going to be at that Planning Commission meeting."

I opened my mouth to deny it, but I could see by the look on her face that she was sitting on some kind of proof. I needed to tread carefully.

"I'm truly sorry, sweetie. I shouldn't have done that. I was trying to save my own tail."

Felicia laughed. "We see how that turned out, since that's where you got shot."

I didn't find that funny at all.

"And now the whole world knows it," I said glumly, tossing aside the *Gazette*. "Guess that's what I deserve."

"That's right," she said. "Want to call it even?"

"Yes, please."

She leaned over and gave me a kiss. The press of her body against mine gave me a sharp pain in the ass.

I probably deserved that, too.